"*May I feed her?*"

Tobie asked.

"Sure." Clay handed her the plate.

At the sight of her dinner, little Molly opened her mouth wide and made sucking noises.

"Are you hungry, sweetheart?" Tobie murmured. "You like that? Yes. Num-num, good."

The sound of Tobie's light, melodic tones sent a shaft of longing straight through Clay's heart. Until this moment he had not realized how much he wanted a wife and baby of his own.

Not now, Barton. Not until he was ready to reveal his true identity to Tobie. But first he had to make sure she would value him for himself and not his money....

Dear Reader,

Welcome to another wonderful month at Silhouette Romance. In the midst of these hot summer days, why not treat yourself (come on, you know you deserve it) by relaxing in the shade with these romantically satisfying love stories.

What's a millionaire bachelor posing as a working-class guy to do after he agrees to baby-sit his cranky infant niece? Run straight into the arms of a very beautiful pediatrician who desperately wants a family of her own, of course! Don't miss this delightful addition to our BUNDLES OF JOY series with *Baby Business* by Laura Anthony.

The ever-enchanting award-winning author Sandra Steffen is back with the second installment of her enthralling BACHELOR GULCH miniseries. This time it's the local sheriff who's got to lasso his lady love in *Wyatt's Most Wanted Wife*.

And there are plenty of more great romances to be found this month. Moyra Tarling brings you an emotionally compelling marriage-of-convenience story with *Marry In Haste*. A gal from the wrong side of the tracks is reunited with the sexy fire fighter she'd once won at a bachelor auction (imagine the interesting stories they'll have to tell) in Cara Colter's *Husband In Red*. RITA Award-winning author Elizabeth Sites is back with a terrific Western love story centering around a legendary wedding gown in *The Rainbow Bride*. And when best friends marry for the sake of a child, they find out that real love can follow, in *Marriage Is Just the Beginning* by Betty Jane Sanders.

So curl up with an always-compelling Silhouette Romance novel and a refreshing glass of lemonade, and enjoy the summer!

Melissa Senate
Senior Editor
Silhouette Romance

Please address questions and book requests to:
Silhouette Reader Service
U.S.: 3010 Walden Ave., P.O. Box 1325, Buffalo, NY 14269
Canadian: P.O. Box 609, Fort Erie, Ont. L2A 5X3

BABY BUSINESS

Laura Anthony

Silhouette

R O M A N C E™

Published by Silhouette Books

America's Publisher of Contemporary Romance

To Jason and Emily. Thanks for the inspiration.

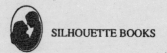

SILHOUETTE BOOKS

ISBN 0-373-19240-1

BABY BUSINESS

Copyright © 1997 by Laurie Blalock

This edition published by arrangement with Harlequin Books S.A.

® and TM are trademarks of Harlequin Books S.A., used under license.
Trademarks indicated with ® are registered in the United States Patent
and Trademark Office, the Canadian Trade Marks Office and in other
countries.

Printed in U.S.A.

Books by Laura Anthony

Silhouette Romance

Raleigh and the Rancher #1092
Second Chance Family #1119
Undercover Honeymoon #1166
Look-Alike Bride #1220
Baby Business #1240

LAURA ANTHONY

started writing at age eight. She credits her father, Fred Blalock, as the guiding force behind her career. Although a registered nurse, Laura has achieved a life-long dream and now pursues writing fiction full-time. Her hobbies include jogging, boating, travel and reading voraciously.

Bundles
of JOY

Dear Reader,

Although I have no children of my own, I was the oldest of
five siblings and learned by proxy what it meant to be a
parent. There are periods of sheer joy punctuated by
occasional moments of feeling completely overwhelmed by
the responsibility.

I was reminded of this while visiting my brother, Jason, and
his nine-month-old daughter, Emily. Jason was installing baby
locks on his kitchen cabinets while Emily crawled under his
feet. She was laughing, cooing, sticking things in her mouth
and generally creating havoc. As I watched the emotions cross
my brother's face—happiness, frustration, exasperation and
fatherly tolerance—a story idea rooted in my mind.

What would happen if I took one eccentric, head-in-the-clouds
bachelor who unexpectedly finds himself in charge of his
sister's baby, and added one practical, feet-on-the-ground lady
doctor? It didn't take long. Soon *Baby Business* was born.

Recently I married my own true-life hero and he turned my
world upside down. Suddenly I found myself thinking
thoughts I'd never before entertained. Thoughts of lullabies,
teddy bears and sweet toothless smiles. At last I truly
understood what makes people want babies. Love. Plain and
simple. And who knows? Maybe someday my husband and I
will have a bundle of joy to call our very own.

Best wishes,

Laura Anthony

Chapter One

"Oh, Clay, the most dreadful thing has happened!"

"What's wrong?" An anxious pang twisted Clay Barton's gut as he stared at his younger sister, Anne. She stood on his front stoop, her nine-month-old daughter, Molly, perched on her hip. Worry lines creased Anne's forehead, and her face was pale.

"It's Holt's mom." Anne hesitated and took a deep breath. "She's got to have emergency surgery, so we're flying out this afternoon to be with her. I'm picking Holt up at the office, but I don't have anyone to look after Molly."

"Come inside." Clay took his sister's arm and led her over the threshold into the little apartment he rented in a modest section of west Fort Worth. With one hand he swept a pile of nuts and bolts from the sofa cushion and gently guided his sister down.

"We can't take Molly with us, she's teething and cranky, and it's too late to call the service and get a nanny today."

Although Holt and his sister had enough money to hire

ten nannies, Clay was proud that Anne had refused to hire a live-in for Molly like most of their well-to-do friends. Of course, at times like this the decision didn't seem so wise.

"Too bad Mom and Dad are in Japan." Clay rocked back on his heels.

Anne shook her head. "If it wasn't such short notice I could find someone. But we'll probably be gone at least three days, maybe longer."

"I'm really sorry to hear about Holt's mother."

"You're my only hope, Clay. If you could just take Molly for today, then the service could get a nanny out tomorrow. And since you're home every day I was praying it wouldn't be too much of an imposition."

Imposition? More like a major life-style change. Clay stared at his niece. Gleefully she kicked her chubby legs. He stroked his chin with a thumb and forefinger, creating a slight rasping sound. The thought of being exclusively responsible for a kid scared the daylights out of him.

Cornered, Clay pursed his lips. How could he turn down his sister in need, yet how could he assume care of an infant? Especially now when he was about to make a breakthrough on his latest invention, the Barton Home Recycling Machine. He'd been burning the midnight oil for weeks hoping to iron out the inevitable glitches. Clay tried to think of a way to extricate himself and failed. After all, it *was* only one day.

"Parenting is out of my league," he hedged.

Anne sighed. "I understand if it's too much for you. I guess Holt will have to go alone."

Clay felt like something nasty on the bottom of a shoe. What the hell. He'd been working on the recycler for four years, what was another day or two? Besides, this was his niece. It would give him good practice for that day far in the future when he became a father.

"I'll do it."

"Oh, Clay, thank you. You don't know how much this means to me and Holt."

"Hey, what are big brothers for?" He chucked Anne under the chin, his gaze traveling to the doe-eyed infant sucking her thumb in his sister's lap. "Let's just hope Molly and I both survive."

"Don't be silly, " Anne said. "You're marvelous with her."

Molly gurgled as if in agreement.

"I brought some of Molly's stuff with me," Anne instructed. "Clothes, formula, diapers, her car seat and stroller. I'm afraid I was pretty frantic so I don't know what I packed, but you can go over to the house for anything else you might need. I was in such a hurry I even forgot to turn on the alarm system."

"Don't worry," he assured her. "I'll take care of everything."

"I wrote up a list of instructions for Molly's daily routine, plus the name of her pediatrician and my permission to have her treated in case something should happen." Anne took a stack of notepaper from her purse and passed it to Clay.

Overwhelmed, his mind whirling with the implications of instant fatherhood, Clay simply nodded. Whew. Alone with a baby. He looked down at his niece again. She wore a frilly, pink dress with white bunnies on the front and gave him a winsome, toothy smile. Heck, he'd kept her a time or two in the past, but never for longer than a couple of hours. He swallowed hard.

"Don't worry." Anne patted his arm, then stood on tiptoes to kiss his cheek. "You'll do fine. I have complete confidence in you."

"Call me as soon as you get there," he said.

"Of course." Anne squatted down in front of Molly. "Bye-bye, snookie bear," she cooed. "You be a good girl for Uncle Clay. Mommy loves you." Anne rained kisses on her daughter's face, then straightened. "No one could ask for a better brother."

She pressed her house key into his hand. He swung Molly onto his hip and walked Anne out the door, down the steps and over to the expensive luxury car parked outside his apartment complex. He helped Anne unload Molly's belongings and set them on the curb.

"Have a safe trip."

Anne kissed them both again, then got into the car. She donned sunglasses and started the engine. Clay couldn't help noticing the tight worry lines around his sister's mouth. He and Molly waved goodbye until Anne's car disappeared from sight, then he glanced at the trusting little soul peeking up at him. Her grin widened and she held out her arms in a gesture so charming it touched Clay's heart.

"Well," he said to Molly, "looks like it's just you and me, kid."

Molly wouldn't stop crying.

Clay was beside himself. He didn't know what to do. He'd given her a bottle, burped her and even fed her bits of his banana when she'd reached for it. He'd changed her diaper, talked to her, rocked her and paced the floor with her. Still, the child wouldn't stop wailing. Huge tears trailed down her reddened face. Her little body shivered from the effects of those gulping sobs.

After several hours, when she showed not the slightest sign of quieting, Clay had to admit defeat. Obviously something was very wrong. He needed professional help. Jostling Molly on his hip, he leafed through the notes Anne had left him until he found the number to the hospital in Little Rock, Arkansas.

He spoke soothingly to the child while he waited for the operator to patch him through to the surgical waiting room, but Molly was having none of it. She arched her back and bucked against him, her cries growing louder, more insistent, until Clay's ears roared with the plaintive sound.

Someone answered in the waiting room but told him neither Anne nor Holt were there. Frustrated, he slammed down the phone. Where were they? Had their plane been delayed? Was Holt's mother in surgery yet?

"Come on, Molly," he begged, "give me a break."

She looked at him with such a desolate expression on her face, Clay immediately felt guilty for his impatience. Maybe the baby was sick. What a terrifying thought. His worst nightmare come to life. Deciding it was better to be safe than sorry, he went back to the telephone and dialed Molly's pediatrician.

"This is Clay Barton, and I need to make an appointment for my niece, Molly Johnson," he said when the receptionist answered the phone. "Now. Today. This afternoon."

"I'm sorry, Mr. Barton, but we're completely booked up today, but I might be able to work her in first thing tomorrow morning."

"And listen to the baby cry like this all night? No way." For emphasis, he held the receiver close to Molly's sobbing mouth, then returned it to his ear. "Hear that?"

"If it's an emergency, sir, you can take her to the hospital."

Clay sighed, thanked the woman and hung up. "Well, Molly, what are we gonna do? Is it an emergency, kiddo?"

Molly quieted a moment, and stared at him. Just when he thought the crisis was over, she hiccuped and started in with a fresh round of tears. Shoot. If only he knew what was wrong. If she were really sick, he wouldn't hesitate to take her to the hospital, but maybe she was just missing her mother.

"Well, there's more than one doctor in this town, isn't there?" He opened the phone book and leafed through it until he found the listing for physicians. Running his finger down the list, he searched for doctors in his neighborhood and started dialing.

After three pediatricians and two family practitioners told him they were too backed up to fit her in, Clay finally lucked out. A Dr. Tobie Avery agreed to see Molly if he could get her to the office within the next half hour.

"Thank God for Dr. Avery," Clay said, hanging up the phone. "He's my kinda man."

He brushed his lips lightly across Molly's fuzzy little head. She smelled so good, like baby powder and innocence. Her eyes drooped, and her sobs lightened to miserable sniffles.

Waltzing her into his bedroom, Clay held his breath, praying that the lapse in crying was permanent. But when he sat her down on his unmade bed, the waterfall of tears returned. Hurriedly he dug through the little suitcase Anne had packed for her and found a yellow sweater and matching bonnet. It was windy outside, and Clay didn't want to take any chances on giving the kid an earache on top of everything else.

Molly squalled the entire time he dressed her, carried her outside and buckled her into her car seat. Clay got behind the wheel and slipped the key into the ignition. The car whined its complaint. He pumped the gas pedal and tried again but his twelve-year-old sedan refused to cooperate. The starter clicked ominously a few times, then nothing.

Swearing under his breath, Clay got out, took Molly back inside and loaded her into the stroller. Good thing Dr. Avery's office was only two blocks away, otherwise he would have to spring for a taxi. There were definite disadvantages to posing as a poor man. He rented a cheap apartment and kept a beat-up car in order to remain incognito. When he'd been Clay Barton, son of one oil and gas magnate Carlton Barton, he'd been deluged with unwanted advances from money-grubbing females. Someone was always trying to marry him.

Four years ago he'd turned his back on the society scene, seeking refuge in the simple life. He enjoyed living like a hermit. Although his family hadn't understood his decision, they respected it. Finally he had the peace and quiet he needed to work on his inventions.

Rapidly propelling the stroller down the sidewalk, Clay cursed his luck. Molly's discomfort kept him from enjoying the warm sun, the bright azure sky and the crisp spring air. He ignored the colorful tulips blooming in a neighbor's narrow window planter, disregarded the puppies playing on the front lawn.

By the time he reached the doctor's office, mounting tension had him ready to pull his hair out, strand by strand.

Dr. Tobie Avery's office was small, and his was the only name on the door. Clay entered the deserted waiting room. Obviously Dr. Avery didn't do a booming business. A receptionist, so young she looked like a high school girl in VOE training, smiled up at him.

"My, that child has a fine set of lungs," said the girl.

"Yeah." Clay nodded, reaching in his pocket for his wallet to retrieve the permission slip Anne had written him. He riffled through the contents but couldn't find the letter. He patted his pockets. No note. With a groan, he realized he'd left it on the dashboard of the car.

Damn. He was either going to have to go back for the permission slip or pretend Molly was his kid. Clay ran a hand through his hair, caught in the quandary. What could it hurt? Dr. Avery wasn't Molly's regular doctor, anyway. No one would ever have to know.

The baby's incessant sobbing was the deciding factor.

"I'm Clay Barton," he said, "and this is my daughter, Molly."

Dr. Tobie Avery heard the baby screaming from her office at the rear of the clinic. She finished the apple that had served as her lunch and tossed the core into the wastebasket. Pushing back from her desk, she got up, washed her hands at the sink, then dried them on a paper towel. The morning had been hectic, and Monday afternoons were her time off to do paperwork, but when her receptionist, Lilly, had told her about the harried man with a crying baby, she'd agreed to see them. Now hearing the child's screams for herself, Tobie understood why the poor man had sounded so distressed.

Tucking a strand of hair behind her ear, Tobie walked down the corridor, opened the door separating the waiting room from the rest of the building and peered out.

A tall lanky man stood at the front desk, a look of pure despair written across his interesting facial features. He clasped a wriggling yellow bundle to his chest. A bundle that possessed a cry as loud as a megaphoned cheerleader at a high school pep rally.

Tobie took instant pity on him. "May I help you?" she asked, stepping across the floor to join him at the front desk.

"Yes. I need to see Dr. Avery right away," he said, relief ringing in his voice at the sight of her. "Molly won't stop crying."

Tobie extended her hand. "I'm Dr. Avery."

The man arched an eyebrow in mild surprise, but quickly took her hand and shook it heartily. His grip was firm, self-confident. His gray eyes sparkled with an intriguing light.

"Sorry, I wasn't expecting..."

"A woman?" Tobie finished the sentence for him.

"Such a young and beautiful woman," he said, valiantly struggling to keep a grasp on the baby.

"Why don't you bring Molly back to the exam room?" Tobie smiled. She was used to that reaction from her patients. Her first name did tend to throw people for a loop.

They generally expected a kind, elderly man, who might have shortened Tobias to Tobie. She ushered them through the door and into the examination room.

"Could you undress your daughter, please?" Tobie asked, closing the door behind them. She'd only been in practice for six months and, so far, couldn't afford to hire a nurse. Taking a glass thermometer from its holder mounted on the wall, Tobie shook it down and waited while he unbuttoned Molly's sweater.

Tobie noticed how tenderly he removed the child's clothing, as if he were afraid she'd shatter into a million pieces. Suddenly she felt jealous of Mrs. Barton, and an odd sense of longing stabbed through her as she thought of her Edward. Somehow she couldn't imagine him caring for a baby at all, much less with tenderness.

That's not fair, she scolded herself. Edward's already raised three children. She had to understand his reluctance in wanting more. They could have a happy life together without children, and who knew, maybe someday she'd convince him to change his mind.

Once Clay had stripped Molly to her diaper, Tobie moved closer and took the child's temperature. Molly's screams intensified during the unpleasant procedure. The man grimaced and looked away.

"Can you tell me what happened?" Tobie asked, once she'd finished examining the baby.

He stuffed his hands into his pockets and hunched his shoulders forward. "She started crying about an hour after her mother left."

"How long ago was that?"

He consulted his watch. "My gosh, she's been crying for three straight hours."

"Did anything precipitate it?"

"What do you mean?"

"Her tummy appears to be a little distended. When was the last time she had a bowel movement?"

He blushed. "I...uh...don't know."

"Did she ingest anything not on her normal diet?"

"I gave her a banana." Clay frowned. "I don't know if Anne normally feeds her bananas or not."

"Why don't you call your wife and find out?"

"Uh..." He hesitated again. "We're not married." For some stupid reason, maybe it was Dr. Tobie's beautiful sable hair or her angelic heart-shaped face or that lithe body that wouldn't quit, but Clay didn't want her thinking he was married.

"That's all right, you don't have to explain your marital status to me. I'm simply trying to determine if Molly has colic." Tobie smiled, and Clay felt as if he'd been shot by an arrow, straight through the heart.

Oh great, Clay thought. Now she'll figure I got some woman pregnant and wouldn't marry her. She must think I'm an A-number-one jerk.

"It could be the bananas, especially if she wasn't used to eating them," Tobie mused, sliding Molly's arm back into her sweater. The child quieted. She hiccuped a few times and sighed.

"You think it's colic?" Clay weaved his fingers together and peered anxiously at Molly.

"Maybe just an old-fashioned tummy ache." Tobie finished dressing the baby and handed her back to Clay. "I'll write you a prescription."

Tobie sat down on a stool, opened the drawer on the exam table and took out a prescription pad. Clay stared, mesmerized by her long, gorgeous legs as she crossed them demurely at the ankle. Her chin-length hair swung like a silk curtain against her pale cheek. The image of Snow White floated into his brain. Dr. Tobie Avery exuded the same delicate beauty, the same sedate self-assurance as the fairy-tale princess. Clay had been in love with Snow White when he was a kid.

"Listen," he said. "I've got to be honest with you."

Dr. Tobie Avery glanced up at him. "Yes?" She had a high clear voice that tinkled like a crystal chandelier rustling in the breeze.

Clay gulped. "I'm not Molly's father."

"I beg your pardon?"

Raising a hand to massage his brow, Clay wished he'd taken the time to go back to the car for Anne's letter. "Molly's my niece not my daughter. I'm watching her while my sister is out of town."

"Oh."

He winced. "I didn't mean to lie to you, but I was desperate."

Tobie stared at him. "Do you realize, Mr. Barton, I'm jeopardizing my license by treating Molly without her mother's permission. I'm not even her regular pediatrician."

"Oh, I've got Anne's written permission. But I left it in the car."

"Then go outside and get it." Tobie looked at him as if he were a backward child.

Good grief, Barton, she thinks you're an idiot.

"Therein lies the problem," he said, attempting to extricate himself.

"Yes?" Dr. Tobie Avery blinked her big blue eyes at him, and Clay held his breath. It had been a very long time since a woman had affected him so physically. He clutched Molly to his chest and realized she'd stopped crying. In fact, her head rested so heavily upon his shoulder, he suspected she'd finally cried herself to sleep.

"My car wouldn't start, so Molly and I walked over."

A smile tugged the corners of Tobie's lips. "Sounds like

you and Molly have had a very trying day, Mr. Barton. It is Mr. Barton, isn't it?''

"Clay."

"It's Mr. Clay?''

"Oh, no. My first name's Clay. Clay Barton. But please, call me Clay,'' he blathered, totally discombobulated by his unexpected attraction to this lady physician. Next, he'd start stuttering the way he had as a kid in the schoolyard. What was it about this woman that left him feeling tongue-tied and shy? It was more than her beauty. When he'd played the part of wealthy bachelor on the loose, he'd had his pick of the most gorgeous women in the Southwest and none of them had ever caused such an unexpected sensation inside him.

"Okay, Clay. Our problem is easily rectified. I'll give you and Molly a lift home, and you can find me that letter of permission for her files. How does that sound?''

"I don't want to put you to any trouble, Dr. Avery,'' Clay said. She does think I'm an idiot, he groaned inwardly.

"No trouble at all. We'll stop by the pharmacy on the way and pick up Molly's prescription.'' She stood up and stepped closer to Clay. Her dainty fragrance teased his nostrils. She smelled sweet, and fresh like a flower. Purple flowers. Violets. That was it. Dr. Tobie Avery smelled like sun-kissed violets.

"Thanks,'' Clay said, surprised to hear his voice come out rough and husky.

"Looks like the little one has fallen asleep,'' Tobie commented, reaching out a finger to lightly stroke Molly's cheek. The wistful longing in her tone told him she had no children of her own but wanted them desperately. She stood so very near, Clay could see the tiny pores on her flawless skin. He trembled slightly and wondered again at the strange chemical reaction seething inside him like a lab experiment gone awry.

"She needs the rest."

"You know, Mr. Barton, it's really sweet of you to take care of Molly for your sister, a lot of men wouldn't do it."

Dr. Avery thought he was sweet. Clay didn't know if that was bad or good. He wanted Tobie to think he was tough and manly, not Mr. Mom. "I didn't have much of a choice. Anne's mother-in-law is having emergency surgery and there wasn't anybody else to look after the baby."

"Your sister is a lucky woman."

"Ah, shucks, Dr. Avery, you're embarrassing me."

"Somehow, Mr. Barton, I doubt that." Her blue eyes flashed with mirth. "You strike me as very self-assured."

"I do?"

"Let me get my keys and I'll drive you home."

Clay followed Tobie back to her office and waited while she hunted in the desk for her purse. He couldn't help admiring the bewitching view as she leaned over. Her satiny peach blouse, only partially hidden by her white lab coat, strained across her generous chest. One well-rounded hip angled provocatively in his direction. Sucking in air, Clay placed a restraining hand to Molly's back and found himself wondering if Dr. Tobie Avery was the sort of woman who favored silky lingerie. Skimpy black lace panties, or maybe a push-up bra? Clay swallowed hard. The woman was wearing an engagement ring, he might as well discontinue his flights of fantasy right now.

"Here we are," she said, straightening, the key dangling in her hand.

"I don't want to keep you from your other patients," Clay apologized. "I hate to be a bother."

Tobie smiled again. "No trouble at all." She noticed how gently he cradled the baby. "Actually it's my afternoon off to do paperwork. I only agreed to see Molly because my receptionist, Lilly, said she was crying loud enough to wake the dead. I hate for children to suffer."

"She's tuckered out."

"You don't have any children of your own, Mr. Barton?" Tobie cocked her head. It was unusual for a man to be so comfortable around an infant that wasn't his. He must have been raised in a large family, she surmised, and felt a stab of sadness. As an only child, she'd dreamed of having siblings to squabble with. If she ever did have kids of her own she'd definitely have more than one. In fact, she wanted half a dozen.

"Me? Oh no! I've never been married."

"You're a natural parent." Completely the opposite of Edward, a nagging voice in the back of Tobie's mind reminded her.

"You should have seen me an hour ago." Clay chuckled. "I was a total basket case."

Tobie liked the sound of his rich, throaty voice. She imagined that voice crooning to her in the middle of the night, and she suppressed a shiver of delight. What was she thinking? She was getting married in six months, why was she having daydreams about strange men?

Especially such an attractive man. Her gaze traveled the length of his body. He was the sort of fellow her grandmother would have called "a tall drink of water." From the scruffy, brown hair, inching past the collar of his bomber jacket, to the tight, faded jeans encasing his long legs, to the five-o'clock shadow ringing his firm jawline. He was one hundred percent fantasy. Patrick Swayze, Mel Gibson and Harrison Ford all rolled into one and then some. The fact that he held a baby in his arms only accentuated his masculinity, vividly contrasting weak with strong.

Stop it right now Tobie Lynne Avery, she scolded herself. She knew better than to let her mind wander along such dangerous lines. Dr. Edward James Bennet III was the man for her. Edward was reliable, secure, dependable. A virtual rock of a man. Just the kind of mate she required.

Tobie need never worry about the future, married to a steady man like Edward.

But what about passion, that nasty little voice nagged. What about physical desire?

In the six months she and Edward had been engaged, he'd never aroused her the way Clay Barton did with a simple smile. Tobie shook her head to dispel her thoughts. She'd sworn never to be swept away by love as her mother had—marrying in the heat of passion, paying for her rash decision every day of her life.

"Are you ready, Mr. Barton?" she asked, putting a professional timbre in her voice.

"Please," he said, "call me Clay."

"Clay, then. This way." Tobie crooked her finger at him and lead him out the back door and through the parking lot to where her late model foreign sports car was parked.

Clay took a gander at the vehicle and whistled. "This must have set you back a pretty penny."

Tobie flushed. "My fiancé bought it for me when I graduated med school. Heaven knows I'm so far in debt on student loans I couldn't have purchased it myself."

"Your fiancé? He must be loaded."

"Edward is financially secure, yes."

Was it her imagination or did she detect a touch of disappointment on Clay Barton's handsomely carved face? Tobie tossed her hair and unlocked the passenger side door, avoiding Clay's inquisitive stare.

"Oh, dear," she said. "I don't have a car seat for the baby."

"It'll be all right." Clay said. Cautious of Molly, he placed a palm to the back of her head as he ducked down and slid into the leather seat. "We only live a couple of blocks away, and I'll buckle the seat belt around both of us."

Tobie got in and backed out of the parking lot. Yes, she

enjoyed the little fire-engine-red sports car Edward had purchased for her. It was a sure sign of his affection. No one in her family had ever owned a new car. She remembered a steady procession of unreliable clunkers probably just like the one Clay Barton drove. He certainly looked like the unreliable type.

Except he was taking care of his sister's baby. That was unusual. It seemed Clay Barton didn't fit any mold.

Old memories rose to the surface of her consciousness. Memories she wanted desperately to forget. Her father had been a dreamer with wanderlust fever, dragging her and her mother from state to state, always on the prowl for a get-rich-quick scheme. They'd never stayed longer than a few months in one place. Tobie had found it difficult to make friends. Her childhood had been one of loneliness and isolation.

Ten years ago her father had died of a heart attack, leaving her mother destitute. During the course of her life, her father had made grandiose promises of fine houses, fast cars and lots of money, but those things had never materialized.

And as much as she had loved her father, he'd never paid her much attention, forever high on his wild ideas. She'd always said whenever she got married she'd pick a solid dependable man. Tobie had realized at a very young age, if she ever wanted anything in life, it was up to her to succeed on her own merits. That goal had driven her to spend her entire adolescence tirelessly studying, making plans to enter medical school from the time she was thirteen. Now, at last, her dreams were coming true. Between her budding medical career and the promise of marrying Dr. Edward Bennet, she'd be assured the stability and security her mother had longed for but never known.

Tobie pulled into the lot across the street, put the car into park and killed the engine. "I'll be right back," she told

Clay, then dashed into the pharmacy to get Molly's prescription filled.

While she waited, Tobie peered through the plate glass window, watching Clay and Molly as they sat in her car. Odd, she thought. They could be a family. A stranger watching them would probably assume that relationship.

"Here you go, Doc," the pharmacist said, ringing up her purchase.

"Thanks," Tobie replied, and paid for the prescription.

What was she doing? This was definitely beyond the call of her Hippocratic Oath, buying medicine for a child who wasn't even her regular patient, giving a ride to a man she didn't know. Something about the pair stirred deep maternal feelings inside her. Besides, if she weren't taking them home, she'd be staring at a stack of paperwork instead, and a few minutes with Clay and Molly was preferable to time alone in her quiet office.

"What's the matter with you?" she muttered under her breath as she pushed through the glass door and stepped back outside into the cool spring air. Normally she loved her job, had never considered it lonely or time-consuming. Did she dare admit the truth to herself? That the handsome man and the darling little girl had roused her maternal instincts. Instincts Edward preferred she ignore.

"Here we go," she said with forced cheerfulness.

"Shh," Clay cautioned. The child resting against his shoulder stirred restlessly and whined in her sleep.

"Well," Tobie said, dropping her voice to a whisper. "At least this time you're armed." She handed him the sack of medicine and snapped her seat belt into place. "Okay, Clay, which direction do you live?"

"Take a left at the stop sign. It's the second set of apartment buildings on your right. I really appreciate you taking time out of your busy schedule to do this for us," he said.

"You're more than welcome." Tobie guided her car

through the light mid-afternoon traffic. "What do you do for a living, Clay, that you can stay home during the day?"

"Umm," he hedged.

Uh-oh, Tobie thought, he's unemployed. She knew it!

"I'm an inventor," he admitted.

Oh, no, even worse than unemployed! Another pie-in-the-sky dreamer, just like her father. Wasn't it a shame all the charming men seemed to have at least one major character flaw? Look at her mother. She'd married her father for love and his devastating good looks, and see where it had gotten her. Thank heavens she'd found a responsible man like Edward. He might not be the sexiest guy alive but he was most certainly steady.

"How do you pay the bills? If you don't mind me asking?"

Clay slid her a look. "Don't worry. I can pay Molly's doctor bill. My check won't bounce."

Tobie had the good grace to look embarrassed. "That isn't what I meant."

Was Tobie Avery the sort of woman who would be impressed with his bank account? She was cool, classy, intelligent. His instincts told him no, that Tobie Avery could see deeper than appearances, but then again she was the same woman who'd accepted a very expensive sports car from her fiancé. He'd had enough dealings with scheming gold diggers to know that fast cars were part of the image.

"To put your mind at ease, I make a little from royalties on an invention I patented two years ago."

"I see."

Yeah. The sudden prim set to her shoulders told him she was measuring his money-making ability, and he'd fallen far short. To the likes of Dr. Tobie Avery, a man following his dreams translated into being a deadbeat. He wondered what she would think if she knew he was really worth millions?

Who was Tobie Avery to judge him? From the way Clay saw it, young Dr. Avery and her well-to-do fiancé deserved each other. Some things mattered more than money. Things like integrity and doing what you loved for a living whether it made big bucks or not.

"This is it," Clay said, indicating his apartment building. He wanted to get back to his sanctuary where he didn't have to face Dr. Tobie Avery's accusing blue eyes.

"Which one?" she asked, sliding him a sidelong glance.

"Second one on the right."

Tobie found a parking space and pulled in. Molly woke, whimpering. Clay undid his seat belt the minute the car stopped and quickly hopped out. Molly fretted, flailed her fists. Clay's hands closed around the paper sack from the pharmacy.

"Thanks, Dr. Avery. Really nice of you to give us a ride home." Anxious to escape, Clay started backing up the sidewalk before Tobie was halfway out of her seat.

"No trouble at all." She smiled, still friendly, but somehow her manner had changed.

The tempo of Molly's cries increased. He needed to get inside. Not only to give Molly her medicine, but to shut the door and create an effective barrier between himself and Dr. Tobie Avery.

Clay fumbled in his pocket for the keys. Molly perched on his right hip, sobbing relentlessly while he searched. He heard the sharp clack-clack of Dr. Avery's high heels on the cement sidewalk, smelled her heady violet aroma as she came up behind him.

Tobie tapped his shoulder. Clay jumped, startling Molly and making her howl louder.

"Why don't you let me hold the baby," she asked. "While you get me that permission-for-treatment letter from Molly's mom." Reaching out, Tobie took the child from his arms.

Clay smacked the side of his head with his palm.
"Anne's note, I completely forgot." This bizarre attraction
he felt for Tobie Avery had befuddled his thinking. "It's
in my car."

Embarrassed, knowing she was watching, Clay made his
way back down to the curb and over to the battered vehicle
that served as his primary mode of transportation. The sedan looked ready for the junk heap, with peeling paint, thin
tires and dented chrome. What a contrast to her sleek, red,
foreign car parked next to it.

He knew in his heart what she had to be thinking. She
probably thought him a thirty-year-old, irresponsible,
washed-out deadbeat. "Drop it, Barton," he growled under
his breath. "Get her the note and then get Dr. Tobie Avery
the hell out of your life, pronto."

Chapter Two

Clay had left the keys swinging in the lock, so Tobie simply opened the door, stepped over the threshold and entered the apartment. She glanced around, surveying her surroundings. Definitely a bachelor's pad. Alien things like springs, hinges and sprockets littered the coffee table along with empty cola cans and potato chip sacks. Sheet metal, welding irons, cathode tubes and strips of rubber decorated the floor. Chips of wood, metal filings and other debris rested on the work bench in the middle of the living room. The place resembled a chemistry lab.

Tobie crossed the room and sank down on the sofa, Molly clutched in her arms. The baby's head wobbled as she gazed up at Tobie. Her breath smelled of sweet milk and infancy. Her chubby cheeks were rosy red and her pale skin felt smooth and soft as fresh butter. Molly's brown eyes widened, then she grinned and Tobie fell instantly in love. The sharp, intense longing zinging through her chest had her gasping.

Oh dear heavens, she wanted a baby! One as dear as this tiny girl.

"Here you go," Clay said, panting. Tobie snapped back from her sudden revelation. His hair was disheveled, his chest heaving as if he'd been running at breakneck speed. He grasped a scrap of paper.

"Thank you." Tobie reached out to take the letter, and her fingers lightly grazed Clay's hand. The results produced more sparks than flint striking flint. Her pulse accelerated at the brief contact. Their gazes met, held with the sticking power of superglue. Tobie sucked in her breath. *He felt it, too!* She recognized the telltale look in his gray eyes. He was experiencing the same mighty yank of sexual attraction as she.

Tobie had just thought him good-looking when she'd inspected him in her office. Now, in the muted afternoon light pouring from the living room window, he was heartbreakingly handsome. From his rough, unshaven jawline to the bold, rugged planes of his cheekbones, to his slightly crooked nose, the man exuded an untamed quality. A quality that excited her and made her want to know him on a more intimate basis.

Her errant thoughts shocked her. What could she be thinking? She was engaged to Edward, and they had never shared an intimate relationship. Her fiancé was very old-fashioned. He had insisted they wait until their wedding night to consummate their marriage, and Tobie willingly agreed. But she should be impervious to other men, no matter how charmingly attractive they might be.

Still, she couldn't drag her eyes from Clay's fascinating face. His lips curved upward, daring her to explore the fine contours with her fingers, her lips, her tongue. She wondered what his mouth would taste like. Sweet nectar? Sharp and salty? Or simply a hot masculine wetness? The thought drove a shudder of longing clean through her spine.

Clay extended his hands and for one tense moment, she thought he was reaching for her, then chagrined, she real-

ized he wanted to take Molly. Dropping her gaze, she surrendered the baby to him.

"Well," she said, folding the letter and sticking it into
the pocket of her lab coat. "I should be going." She got
to her feet and clasped her hands together.

"Thanks again, Dr. Avery, for all your help."

"You're welcome. I hope Molly feels better soon." She
glanced at the baby and smiled. "Call me if you need anything else."

"I will." Clay followed her to the door.

"Goodbye." Tobie waved, then hurried down the stairs,
her heart pounding at an alarming rate. Her hands trembled
as she unlocked her car and climbed inside.

What on earth is happening to me? she wondered, and
bit her bottom lip. Time to get back to her office and firmly
put thoughts of babies and Clay Barton far from her mind.

"Good night, Lilly."

"Good night, Dr. Avery. See you tomorrow."

"Be careful going home." Tobie looked up from her
desk and slid a fountain pen behind her ear.

"Oh." Lilly paused. "I forgot to tell you, that good-
looking hunk that came in this afternoon left his baby
stroller here."

"He did?"

"I stuck it in the corner." Lilly pointed at the yellow
and pink stroller parked off to one side.

"Thanks. You can call Mr. Barton in the morning and
let him know where it is. I'm sure he'll be missing it."

"Sure thing." Lilly grinned, slipping her arms through
her sweater. "Don't work too late."

"I'm almost finished here. I'm going out tonight."

"With Dr. Bennet?"

"Uh-huh."

"Have a good time." Lilly headed out the back door.

Tobie leaned back in her swivel chair and stared at the gaily colored stroller in the corner. There was really no reason to wait until tomorrow to return it. She could drop it off on her way home. It wasn't out of the way, and with Clay's car not working, he might truly need it before morning.

This isn't just a ploy to see Clay again, is it? a suspicious voice in the back of her mind scolded.

"No way," she answered herself out loud and shook her head. She was merely being neighborly.

The telephone rang. Tobie leaned over and snagged the receiver off the hook.

"Hello," Edward's voice, so solid and reassuring, traveled the phone lines, grounding her to reality. "What time do you want me to pick you up?"

"I'm sorry, Edward." Tobie tugged off her clip-on earring and tucked the receiver under her chin. "I forgot when the benefit dinner started."

"Eight o'clock, dear. You don't have much time to change."

Tobie took the pen from behind her ear and tapped it restlessly on her desk. She didn't really want to go to this thing, but it meant so much to Edward. Unfortunately, he attended about ten of these affairs a month and expected her to accompany him to each and every one. There was a definite downside to being engaged to a man so much in the political limelight.

"Edward, I'll be running a little late. I've got to stop and see a patient on the way home."

"Tobie," he chided, clicking his tongue. "I've warned you about getting your patients started on house calls. Do it once and they'll be expecting you to come charging over in the middle of the night for every minor cough or sniffle. You've got to learn to stand firm."

"I'm sure you're right, Edward." She sighed. "But this will only take a few minutes."

"I can't be late, you know. I am the guest speaker."

His tone rubbed her the wrong way. Lately a lot of things about Edward had been rubbing her the wrong way.

"I tell you what, why don't you just go on ahead."

"What? Arrive without an escort?" He sounded as if she'd just suggested he walk naked into a crowded room. Sometimes Edward could be quite stuffy about proper etiquette.

"I'll meet you there. That way you won't have to come halfway across town to pick me up."

"Well." He paused. "I suppose that might work out for the best."

"See you at eight then. The Sid-Richardson Pavilion, right?"

"That's correct."

They said goodbye and hung up. Tobie collected her purse and Molly's stroller. Looking at her watch, she estimated she had just enough time to drop off the stroller, make it home to change and then get back to the medical district by eight o'clock. A tight schedule was good. She wouldn't have time to linger at Clay Barton's place.

She locked up the building and stepped outside into the cool evening air. It wasn't yet daylight saving time and already the vapor street lamps had come on against the gathering darkness. She loaded Molly's stroller in the trunk and drove the short distance to Clay's apartment complex.

For some strange reason her pulse skipped erratically as she walked up the sidewalk, pushing Molly's stroller ahead of her. Too much caffeine, she diagnosed, knowing that wasn't the truth.

She knocked on the door, and when there wasn't an immediate answer, she almost turned and fled. Gathering her courage, she knocked again.

If he doesn't answer within fifteen seconds, I'll leave, she told herself.

At that moment the door was flung inward. Clay stood there shirtless, wearing only a pair of tight blue jeans. Tobie hitched in her breath at the sight of his firm, well-muscled chest. Even his bare feet looked good. Hubba-hubba. Obviously the man spent some time at the gym. His hair stuck out in all directions as if he'd been repeatedly raking his fingers through it. He stared at her and blinked.

"Dr. Avery?"

"I brought back Molly's stroller." She offered him a timid smile. "You left it at the office."

"Thank God you're here." He grabbed her arm and tugged her inside.

"What's the matter?" He didn't have to answer, Tobie heard for herself Molly's deep, racking sobs.

"I gave her some of that medicine and it worked for a little while. She even slept an hour or so. But then a few minutes ago she woke up crying again. Dr. Avery, I'm desperate. I don't know what to do."

Her heart went out to him. The poor man, left all alone with a tiny baby. She peeled off her lab jacket and draped it over the sofa. Following the sound of Molly's cries, she went down the hall and into Clay's bedroom.

Molly stood in a playpen, her little hands gripping the rails so tightly her fingers were white. Tears streamed down her face. She wore footed pajama's and her fuzzy curls mirrored Clay's frustrated hairdo.

"There, there," Tobie cooed, moving to the playpen and lifting Molly into her arms. "You miss your mommy, don't you?"

Clay stood in the doorway behind her, his arms folded across that magnificent chest, his head cocked to one side as he studied them. Tobie gulped and looked away, purposefully focusing all her attention on the baby. Cradling

Molly, Tobie started humming a lullaby. The child quieted almost instantly.

"It's tough," she said, "for a little one to be away from her momma."

"Even tougher on me," Clay grumbled. "I feel useless."

"Oh, no." Tobie shook her head. "You're doing a fine job."

"You really think so?"

"Much better than most. Few men would even agree to keep an infant. Your sister is a lucky woman."

Their gazes met. Tobie noticed his eyes had turned a darker shade of gray, more steel-colored now, but not at all harsh. Her glance trailed down his face, caught and paused at his mouth. She wondered what it would feel like to have those lips on hers. Would he kiss like Edward? Solid, perfunctory? Or would his kisses be wilder, more freewheeling? Would they be long and lingering? Honeyed and sultry? Tobie gulped at the warm, melting sensation in her stomach.

The phone rang, shattering the moment.

"Be right back," Clay said, and disappeared down the hall.

"Yes, ma'am," Tobie crooned to the baby. "You just wanted someone soft to hold you, didn't you darling."

Molly stuck her fist in her mouth and gnawed.

"Are you hungry? Bet old Uncle Clay doesn't know how often to feed a baby, does he? Come on, sugarfoot, let's go find some food."

The affection she felt for this baby surprised Tobie. She worked with children all day long and had never experienced such intense maternal stirring. Maybe it had something to do with the fact she'd just turned twenty-nine. Or maybe it had started two weeks ago when Edward had told her he didn't want any more children.

Because of her intense drive and desire to become a doctor, Tobie had planned to postpone motherhood until her thirties. She'd wanted to establish her practice before she took time off to raise a family. But deep in her heart, she'd always wanted children. Then Edward had sprung his decision upon her. She'd kept hoping of course it was a negotiable issue. She was sure she could change his mind.

Tobie wandered into the kitchen to find Clay leaning against the cabinet, one bare foot lightly resting on the other, the phone tucked into the crevice between his ear and chin. "Yes, Anne, Molly's doing absolutely fine."

Tobie raised her eyebrows at him and he shrugged.

"No. Don't you worry about a thing here. I'm handling it. Yes. Right. Now you get some rest, too. I promise I'll call you if anything happens. Yes. No. Goodbye." Clay recradled the receiver.

"Jeez." He sighed and ran a hand through his hair. "Holt's mom isn't doing well. They had to put her in ICU overnight. Looks like Holt and Anne are going to have to stay longer than they thought."

"Is that why you didn't tell her about Molly?" Tobie asked, opening the refrigerator and looking for baby formula. She spied a can and placed it on the counter.

"What was I suppose to say? Oh by the way, Anne, while you're agonizing over your mother-in-law, I'm losing my mind here with your daughter. I don't know if I can survive this temporary fatherhood gig."

"Here," Tobie said, pulling a can of beer off the six-pack ring she retrieved from the fridge and tossing it to him. It was obvious Molly had taken her toll on Clay. "Go sit down, turn on the TV and put your feet up. Relax. Oh, yeah, and put on a shirt while you're at it."

"Why?" He grinned. "Does it bother you to see my manly chest?"

"Of course not," she lied. Hot and bothered was more

like it. "I don't want you to catch a cold. Then who would take care of Molly?"

His smug grin widened, and Tobie could see she wasn't fooling him a bit. "Okay," he agreed. "For you."

While Clay went to the bedroom for his shirt, Tobie heated the formula in a saucepan then tested the temperature on her bare forearm before pouring it into a plastic bottle. The baby made sucking noises at the sight.

"You are hungry, aren't you little one?" Tobie nestled Molly into the crook of her arm and settled the rubber nipple into her greedy mouth. The baby clamped her hands eagerly around the plastic bottle.

Clay came back into the room, casually tugging a white cotton T-shirt down over his distracting biceps. Tobie breathed a sigh of relief at seeing his exceptional physique properly covered.

He popped the top on his beer and strolled into the living room. He smoothed his hair with one hand, found the remote control and flipped on the TV with the other. Tobie, still feeding Molly, joined him on the sofa.

"I called for a pizza just before Molly woke up. Wanna join me?" he asked, taking a sip of beer. "Buying you dinner is the least I can do for all the trouble I've put you through today."

"That's a really nice offer but I've got to be going." Tobie sneaked a peek at her watch. Seven-fifteen. She wouldn't have time to go home and change now. Edward would be disappointed to see her in working clothes, but that couldn't be helped.

A knock at the door heralded the arrival of the pizza boy.

Clay set his beer on the coffee table, got up and fished in his pocket for money. When he opened the door and exchanged cash for the cardboard box, Tobie caught a whiff of the delicious pepperoni and green pepper aroma. Her favorite. Edward never ordered pizza. He claimed it was a gastronomical horror.

Clay opened the lid, purposefully waving the cardboard to waft the scent her way. "Sure you won't join me? I can't eat it all," he said temptingly. "Come on. One slice won't kill you."

"Well..." Tobie hesitated. Her stomach growled. She'd had two slices of toast for breakfast and an apple for lunch, and right now the pie smelled tantalizing wonderful.

"You're gonna make me eat alone?" he challenged.

"Maybe just one small slice but then I really have to go."

"I knew you'd weaken." Clay winked.

Molly sucked the bottle dry. Her eyelids drooped. Tobie brought the baby to her shoulder and gently patted her back.

"You're good with Molly, too," he said, setting the pizza box down on the coffee table in front of them, then settling himself on the sofa next to Tobie.

"So are you."

"Strange, neither one of us have kids."

"I want some one day."

"Me, too," Clay said. "Or at least I thought I did until I spent a day with that little pistol. 'Course I've got to find the right woman first." He leaned over and affectionately ruffled Molly's hair. The baby grinned at him. "Hey, finally gonna give me a smile?"

Molly held out her arms and Clay took her, bouncing the baby on his knee. Unable to bear the temptation of the pizza any longer, Tobie took a slice from the box.

"Hey, no fair starting without me," Clay teased.

"You're the one with the baby in your lap. Haven't you ever heard? Parents do not get to eat an uninterrupted meal for at least two years."

"Ha!" Clay got up, took Molly to the swing in the corner, buckled her in and wound the thing up. "Pop goes the Weasel" played while Molly swung back and forth. Clay came back, sat cross-legged in the floor at Tobie's feet and helped himself to a slice.

"Umm," Tobie said. It had been a long time since she'd had a pizza. Well over a year ago. Before she'd started dating Edward.

"You got a hot date tonight or what?" Clay asked.

"Nothing like that." Tobie shook her head. "My fiancé is speaking at a political fund-raiser for the AMA."

Clay made a face. "Politics. Yuck." He could well imagine Dr. Tobie Avery's upwardly mobile fiancé. Good-looking no doubt, with impeccable manners. Controlled. A mover and shaker. Clay knew the type. Heck, his folks had wanted him to be the type. The fiancé was probably the perfect mate for the accomplished young woman perched on the edge of his sofa. Clay had never been impressed by the society world, but he *was* impressed by Dr. Tobie Avery. He appreciated the way she'd so willingly come to his rescue with Molly.

"I agree," Tobie said. "But Edward is very involved in politics, and I don't want to disappoint him."

"Sounds like you guys don't have much in common." How could a woman as fine as Dr. Tobie disappoint any man? Clay wondered, suddenly very conscious of her slender legs lurking inches from his arm.

"We have a lot in common," Tobie protested, hastening to correct him.

"Such as?" What wicked elf prompted him to goad her? The odd pinch of jealousy rippling in his chest surprised Clay.

"Uh…" Tobie blinked. "Well, we're both doctors. Although he's a plastic surgeon, and I'm just a family practitioner."

"Yeah, but that's career stuff. What do you guys do for

fun together?'' Clay watched her face and wondered who
Tobie was trying to convince, him or herself.

"Edward and I both enjoy the ballet and gourmet cooking.''

Clay looked at the half-consumed pizza in her hand.
"Not exactly haute cuisine is it?"

"Oh, I didn't mean anything derogatory about the pizza.
It's delicious. In fact, I adore pizza. I haven't eaten any in
such a long time, I was savoring the taste.''

"Old Ed doesn't like pizza, huh?''

That got a smile out of her. "He *hates* to be called Ed.
And how did you know he was older?"

"A guess.''

"Oh.''

"How much older?'' He couldn't resist asking.

"Sixteen years.''

"Since he is your fiancé, I'll refrain from the geriatric
jokes.'' Clay could see why Edward would want a beautiful
woman like Tobie on his arm. What plastic surgeon
wouldn't kill for a wife so gorgeous? It would certainly do
wonders for his business. What Clay couldn't figure out
was why a pretty young woman would pick such a staid
older man for a life partner. Had to be some sort of father
complex, he diagnosed.

Tobie nibbled on her pizza. A dot of tomato sauce rested
on her chin. Clay suppressed the urge to lean over and kiss
the sauce away. Jeez, what was he thinking? Dr. Tobie
Avery was engaged. Not only that, but he couldn't afford
to get involved with any woman. Not now. Not before one
of his inventions paid off. Once he'd proven himself, then
he could daydream about a wife and kids, until that day he
was flying solo. By that time Tobie would be long married
with a half dozen kids in tow. But she was exactly the kind
of woman he was looking for, independent, successful,

good with children. Not to mention attractive, intelligent and downright sexy.

"Molly's out like a light." Tobie nodded at the baby.

"Huh?" Clay blinked, pulling his whimsical thoughts back to the present. "Oh, yeah, she is."

"I better be going."

"Thanks again for your help." Clay unfurled his legs and got to his feet.

"I need to wash up." Tobie finished her pizza and held up her palms.

"Oh, sure. Hey, I'll show you my no-drip faucet. I've got one for every sink."

Tobie heard the pride reverberate in his voice. He was serious about this inventing stuff. Of course her father had been serious about his fly-by-night schemes, as well. Tobie closed her eyes briefly, remembering one particular fiasco which had involved gold mining on an Indian reservation. Her father had lost the family's rent money on that deal, and they'd ended up living in a campground tent for three months.

Sighing, she got up and followed Clay into the kitchen. He turned on the faucet and began describing the design.

"See," he said, "there's no internal washers. Completely unnecessary with the Barton No-Drip Faucet. Since there are no washers, they can't wear out. Guaranteed no drips for life." He turned the faucet off and on several times for effect. "I'm working on bigger things now."

"You expect to be an inventor for the rest of you life?"

Clay arched his eyebrows in surprise. "Why, sure. Inventing is my life. Love me, love my inventions."

Where had she heard that nonsense before? Tobie shook her head.

"What?"

"Don't you think that's a little unrealistic?" He was just

like her father, living in a dream world until the end of his days.

"No." Clay crossed his arms over his chest in a defensive stance.

"How do you ever expect to support a family on an inventor's unreliable income?"

He hesitated a moment, as if he were about to tell her something, then he shrugged. "When I have children, they'll be provided for."

"Thank heavens for that. Spare the poor kids the agony of living in poverty."

"Excuse me?" Clay looked downright hurt. "What's that suppose to mean?"

"Never mind." How many times had she witnessed her parents arguing over this same issue? Daddy's fantasies versus putting food on the table. Her father had never understood the necessity of living in the real world and apparently neither did Clay Barton.

"No." He reached out and touched her elbow. "I want to hear it. What's on your mind, Doctor?"

Tobie stared into those gray eyes and felt herself losing all sense of direction. Inventors should look like Albert Einstein with wild hair and mismatched socks, or a nerdy scientist with pocket protectors and thick black glasses, not like Marlon Brando in *The Wild Bunch.*

She had to admit she'd never met a man quite so alive with pure physical energy. He stepped closer, and Tobie's nerves hummed as if she'd downed a pot of strong coffee.

"You think I'm a bum, don't you?"

"No...not at all."

Tobie gulped. She could see each dark hair of his five-o'clock shadow. His mouth turned up in a sarcastic curl. Suddenly the man, who minutes before had ministered tenderly to a young baby, seemed as deadly as downed power lines. What was she doing here? Why was she so drawn to him?

His fingers dug into her skin, firm but not hurting. Goose bumps skittered up her arm. Her whole body tingled with strange sensations she couldn't name.

"I'm going to patent a successful invention someday," he promised, a hard glint in his eyes. "You'll see."

"You have nothing to prove to me."

"Don't I?"

"No." Tobie ducked her head, desperate to escape the intensity of his gaze. "I'm nothing to you."

His hand left her elbow and moved to her chin. With a finger he tilted her face up to his.

Was he going to kiss her? Tobie's heart thrummed at the prospect. Shocked, she realized how much she wanted to taste him.

His finger moved upward, gently tracing first her cheek, then her lips. Tobie waited, her breath bated. Would he kiss her?

"Too bad," he said at last, his face so close to hers she could smell the aroma of pizza on him.

"Too bad what?" she whispered.

"Too bad you don't consider me good enough to kiss you, Dr. Tobie Avery." He tucked a strand of her hair behind her ear and Tobie feared she might faint. "Imagine the connection we could make."

He dipped his head lower until his lips hovered millimeters from hers.

"I don't think you're not good enough," she denied.

"Oh no?" His eyes glimmered ashy gray with emotions. "Then why don't you kiss me?"

She looked at that mouth. How she wanted to meld with him. He waited, one hand on her chin, the other at her waist.

"I can't," she said. "I'm engaged to another man."

"Are you?"

Puzzled, she shook her head. "What?"

"Are you engaged to a man or just what he can offer you?"

"Excuse me?"

Clay released her and stepped back, leaving Tobie feeling bereft and aching for that promised kiss. When the beeper in her pocket went off, she scarcely noticed.

"You've got a call," he said.

"What? Oh." She pulled her beeper from her pocket and peered at the numbers illuminated on the little black box. The number to Edward's car phone. "Umm, could I use the phone."

Clay gestured at the telephone mounted on the wall. "Be my guest."

Tobie moved over and picked up the receiver, Clay close on her heels. He stood so near her shoulder, Tobie could feel his breath catching the outer rim of her ear. A shiver passed through her. For one disorienting moment, Tobie wondered who she was calling and why.

Edward's voice shook her from the stuporous state induced by Clay Barton's propinquity. "Tobie? Where are you? Are you okay?"

"Yes, Edward, I'm fine." Relief rushed through her like the March winds gusting outside the window. How glad she was she had not succumbed to the wild passions beating in her breasts and kissed Clay Barton. It would have been very foolhardy.

"Well then, may I ask where you are? It's five minutes until eight and I'm sitting in the parking lot outside the Sid-Richardson Pavilion waiting on you." His intonation told her he was irritated.

"I'm sorry, Edward, I got tied up with this house call."

"Didn't I warn you?"

"Yes." Tobie sighed.

Clay reached out and touched her shoulder. Tobie jumped and shied away. "Hang up on him," he whispered. "And stay here with me instead. We can finish the pizza and watch *Casablanca* on the late movie."

His offer tempted her more than he would ever know. *Casablanca* was her favorite movie. Tobie shut her eyes and swallowed hard; her skin burned feverishly hot from Clay's touch.

"Tobie? Did you hear me? Are you still there?" Edward sounded downright peevish.

"I'm here, Edward."

"I thought I heard a man's voice in the background."

"You did, Edward. That's Mr. Barton. His little girl is sick."

"You tell Mr. Barton you have an important engagement to keep and get over here right away. I hate lurking about in parking lots almost as much as I hate entering a gathering without an escort."

"Yes, Edward. I'm on my way."

"Hurry, dear. Goodbye."

He rang off before she had a chance to respond. Had Edward always been so demanding?

"My little girl, huh?" Clay teased.

"Shut up," Tobie snapped, not in the mood to put up with him, either. Men. Give them an inch and they thought they owned you.

"Whoa!" Clay laughed and held up his palms. "Did I get you in trouble with Big Daddy?"

"Where do you get off talking to me like that?" Tobie exploded. "I came here to help you, and now you're treating me like I'm one of your little girlfriends."

"Hey," Clay said, "it was your idea to bring the stroller over."

"What are you suggesting?" she demanded, sinking her hands onto her hips.

"Nothing. Go. Have a good time. Thanks for your help with Molly." Clay ushered Tobie out of the kitchen and through the living room. "Don't worry about me, Dr. Avery, I won't be bothering you again."

"Fine." She responded heatedly, but it wasn't Clay she was angry with nor was it Edward. The seething emotions startled her. What did it mean? She had only herself to blame.

"Good night, Mr. Barton." With that she scooped up her lab coat and stalked out of the house.

Chapter Three

Clay Barton wedged in her mind like a diamond in a ring setting. For the past eighteen hours she'd been unable to think of anything else but the handsome, seductive inventor who'd unintentionally knocked her world out of kilter. Tobie sat behind her desk, staring into a cup of wicked black coffee and trying to shake the fog from her brain. She hadn't slept.

The political dinner had passed in a blur with Tobie smiling appropriately and shaking all the right hands. Edward had been pleased to the point of murmuring to her that he'd never seen her so captivating, but while she'd dined on caviar and lobster and talked with powerful lobbyists for the AMA, her mind had been on Clay Barton, knowing he was eating pepperoni and green pepper pizza, watching *Casablanca* and caring for baby Molly. Tobie would have given anything to be back in that simple apartment snuggling on the sofa with them, instead of at the stuffy, crowded reception hall locked on Edward's arm.

When Edward had kissed her good-night on the steps of

her condo, she couldn't help wishing it was Clay's lips pressed against hers. Such wild, illogical thoughts frightened her. She'd only known Clay Barton for one day and here she was fantasizing about kissing him while she kissed her fiancé. Yet there was no denying the swarm of feelings Clay agitated inside her. The man possessed an intense amount of passion. It showed in the way he carried himself, the way he spoke about his work, the way he tenderly cared for the baby.

Damn. Tobie slammed her fist on her desk. She simply had to cease torturing herself. Obviously she was suffering from a case of animal lust. A mere chemical reaction. Nothing more serious than that. Even if she physically desired Clay Barton she most certainly would not act upon that sensation. She was famous for her cool, calm demeanor under pressure.

However, her inexplicable attraction to a stranger caused Tobie to question her commitment to Edward. How could she marry him when she hungered for another man?

Tobie twirled Edward's two-caret diamond engagement ring on her finger. They'd been engaged six months, had dated another six before that. Edward had the capacity to make her dreams come true. Dreams of stability and dependability. She'd never have to go hungry or wear worn-out clothes. People would no longer laugh at her behind her back. Unlike her irresponsible father, Edward could provide for her. Dare she throw it away for nothing?

But did she love Edward?

The thought caught her in the throat. Tobie closed her eyes. She had thought so, or rather had tried to convince herself that she did. Especially after Edward had asked her to marry him. She'd been giddy as a teenager, excited, thrilled, touched that he wanted a destitute girl from the wrong side of the tracks.

But love?

Tobie swallowed past the lump choking off her airway. What did love mean, anyway? Sentimental words? Overwrought emotions? Her mother had been madly in love with her father, and it had led her into a life of hard toil and sorrow.

Pushing back from her desk, Tobie got to her feet. She paced the floor, her arms folded around her. What to do?

If only Clay Barton hadn't come barreling into her life with that cute child in his arms she would not be having these doubts. She'd probably never see Clay again. She couldn't let a momentary attraction divert her from her real goals.

What were her goals? A thriving family practice, a nice home, a husband. And children. Tobie gulped and tucked a strand of hair behind her ear. Edward didn't want children.

"Dr. Avery?" Lilly's voice crackled over the intercom. "Your nine-o'clock appointment is here."

Tobie stepped back to the desk, pressed down the intercom button. "Thanks, Lil. I'll be right there."

Sliding her lab jacket off the back of the chair, Tobie shook her head. Nothing had to be resolved this minute. She had time to think, to make the correct decision, but for now she had patients waiting.

Tobie shrugged into her lab coat, squared her shoulders, took a deep breath, slid Edward's ring off her finger and dropped it into her pocket. Yes. She had plenty of time.

"Come on, Molly, quit chewing on my shoe." Clay reached over and gently pulled his sneaker from the child's mouth. Molly grinned, drool glistening on her cheek. "I know it's tasty but I don't think Dr. Avery would approve of the germ factor."

Dr. Tobie Avery. A delectable dame who could give Ingrid Bergman a run for her money. Clay blew out a long breath through clenched teeth. What was it about the woman that had so captured his interest? Sure, she was attractive with those well-shaped gams and that silky curtain of sleek black hair, but so what? He spotted attractive women every day of the week, and they didn't twist his guts into knots like electrical wiring in a homemade pipe bomb.

"Big deal. Forget it." Analyzing his feelings made Clay uncomfortable. He could readily dissect mechanical things all day long but when it came to emotions, he preferred the head-in-the-sand method. His motto: if you ignore something long enough it will go away. Like the erotic sensations Dr. Tobie Avery ignited inside him, more combustible than oxygen and gasoline.

Molly looked up at him and cooed.

"You're gonna be a heartbreaker, too, aren't you?" Clay chucked a finger under the baby's chin and was delighted by her outburst of laughter. "Just don't marry for security like a certain doctor we could name." That was unfair, a niggling voice in the back of his mind accused. For all he knew Tobie Avery was madly in love with her old man fiancé. So why had she brought Molly's stroller back to the apartment last night and why had she almost let him kiss her?

"Guess I'm destined to be another Rick, huh?" Clay ran a hand through his hair and eyed the baby, sitting in her walker.

Molly gurgled.

"You're right. Too much *Casablanca*. Remind me to stick with Rambo movies."

Clay settled back on his well-worn, plaid sofa and picked up the conglomeration of cogs and gears that served as the internal guts to his recycling machine. He'd gone over to Anne and Holt's house for more baby supplies and to get the number for the nanny service, but he hadn't gotten around to making the call yet. He'd been too preoccupied playing catch up for missing yesterday's work. Because his place was a virtual baby land mine, he'd had to stash Molly in her walker.

Hard rock music blasted from stereo speakers but Molly didn't seem to mind. In fact, the kid nodded her head in time to the throbbing beat.

He looked around his haphazard apartment and grinned. Ah, a man's domain. No lace curtains or pink bedspreads here. No fluffy things on the toilet seat. Only bare necessities and lots of testosterone. Wonder what Dr. Tobie had thought of his apartment?

She hated it, he decided, and grinned to himself. Right down to the stuffed moose head mounted on the wall. The telephone rang.

Clay scrambled around in the sofa cushions for the remote control and turned the stereo down a decibel. "Don't go anywhere, little girl," he chided and shook a finger at Molly. "And lay off the sneakers." He kicked his shoes out of her reach and padded to the kitchen on bare feet.

"Hello?"

"Clay? It's Anne."

"Hey, sis, how's your mom-in-law?"

"Not good."

He heard the clear signs of stress in her terse reply. "Ah. I'm sorry to hear that."

"We're going to have to stay in Little Rock longer than we expected. Maybe a whole week."

A whole week? Yikes. Clay placed his palm to his forehead.

"Clay? You still there?"

"Sure, sis."

"Has the nanny arrived yet?"

"Uh, well, I forgot to call."

"How are you doing with Molly?"

"Just fine. We're having a good time."

"I'm glad everything is all right, but since we're going to be gone longer than expected you better call the service now. If you wait too late you won't be able to get anyone out today," his sister admonished.

"Okay."

"Thank you, Clay. You don't know how much this means to me."

"No prob."

"How is my precious angel? Is she being good?"

"Perfect."

Anne breathed a sigh. "You're one in a million, brother. I'll never be able to repay you."

"Just worry about taking care of Holt's mom, and we'll see you when we see you."

"I'll call again tomorrow," Anne promised, then hung up.

Clay strolled back to the living room. "That was your ma, Miss Molly Malone," he said, then noticed that the baby had managed to inch her walker over to the coffee table. "Hey! What have you been up to?"

Molly looked up at him, a guilty expression on her face and a grayish stain around her mouth. She had something clutched tightly in her fist.

Instant terror struck his heart. "Molly, what have you got?" Clay leapt over the sofa to get to her faster. He reached down and grasped her hand in his. "Let me see."

Molly howled. When she opened her mouth, Clay saw the same gray stain on her tongue.

Oh, God.

Frantically Clay unfisted her little fingers and stared down at the thin wire filament resting in her palm. He took it away from her and stuck it in his pocket.

His pulse raced hotter than a thermonuclear reaction. Panic charged through him. What to do?

Molly shrieked at the top of her lungs. Was she in pain? How much had she swallowed? A flood of terrible scenarios rushed through his mind. What if the wire threads lacerated her throat? What if she had to have surgery? What if ingesting the metal proved fatal? God, he should have hired a nanny!

Without stopping to think, Clay jerked her out of her walker and started for the door. Only his bare feet hitting the cool pavement on the front porch, brought him back inside long enough to jam his feet into his sneakers. He took off again, untied shoelaces flapping around his ankles.

With Molly tucked securely into the curve of his elbow like a football, Clay sprinted the few blocks to Tobie Avery's office. He burst through the door, his lungs heaving great gulps of air.

"Where's Dr. Avery?" he shouted at Lilly. "I've got an emergency here!"

Lilly's eyes grew wide as pickle jar lids, she got up from her chair. "What's the matter, Mr. Barton."

"I have to see Dr. Avery. Now."

"Just a minute." Lilly disappeared through the door behind the receptionist's desk.

Clay's gaze swept through the waiting room. Several people stared at him curiously. He must look like a crazy man, with his hair wild, his rapid breathing and untied shoelaces. Molly's hot tears splashed on his bare arm. Clay lifted her up and brought her to his shoulder. "Hurry," he muttered. "Hurry."

Tobie followed Lilly into the lobby. She hadn't expected to see Clay Barton ever again and certainly not today. Lilly's description of his panicked state had Tobie abandoning the elderly lady with a chronic cough in exam room one in order to see exactly what was going on.

She stepped through the door and her eyes met Clay's.

Stark fear was reflected in those stormy gray depths. She held a hand out to him.

"Please," she said calmly, "come on back."

"Tobie," he said, his voice strangled with emotion. "Molly's swallowed something."

She placed an arm across Clay's shoulders, intending to comfort him. Instead, her own body reacted to the contact as if she had a raging fever. Perspiration broke out on her forehead. Her mouth went dry. Heat swamped her body, followed immediately by an icy chill. She moved away from Clay and her disturbing symptoms started to abate.

"Tell me what happened?" Her own voice shook as she ushered them into exam room two.

"I had Molly in my living room," Clay began, sitting the baby on the examining table. Tobie noticed his hands trembled, his face blanched pale. The baby had quieted and stared at Tobie with interest. "I was working on my recycling machine."

"Yes?" Tobie urged, struggling hard to regain her professional composure.

"I didn't want her getting into all that stuff I use in my inventions, so I put her in her walker where I could keep an eye on her." Clay's breathing slowed as he collected himself. "Whew. Is it hot in here or is it just me?"

"You've been through a trying experience. Calm down, breathe deeply, then continue." Tobie leaned against the exam table, her clinical gaze raking over Molly's little body for any signs of problems.

Clay jabbed a hand through his hair. "The phone rang. It was Anne. I only left Molly for a few minutes, but when I came back…" He gestured helplessly at the baby. "She'd scooted her walker over to my work bench." He closed his eyes as if reliving the moment and swallowed so hard Tobie could see his Adam's apple bob in response.

"Yes?"

"She had that gray stuff all over her mouth and tongue and this iron filament in her hand." Clay dug the thready piece of metal from his pocket and passed it over to Tobie.

Tobie looked at it. "Iron, you say?"

"Yes."

"Hmm." Tobie pressed her lips together.

"Is she going to be okay?"

"Is there anything else she might have swallowed?"

Clay nodded. "Could be anything. There's bits of wood and paper and rubber all over the place. I wouldn't even know if anything was missing."

Tobie took her stethoscope from her pocket, bent over and laid it on the baby's chest. Molly chortled in response. Tobie listened for several minutes then straightened.

"Well?"

"Her airway sounds clear. Her color is good. Obviously nothing got stuck on the way down."

"And?" Clay clasped his hands together and looked as nervous as any father would under the same circumstances.

Tobie shrugged. "If she did swallow something, it'll probably pass through without a problem."

"Is that it?"

"I could X-ray her stomach."

Clay nodded. "Yeah. Do that."

"You're not even certain she swallowed anything for sure are you? The gray residue on her mouth might simply be from sucking on the iron filament. The X-ray might be completely unwarranted."

Clay's mouth twitched with indecision. "What do you think?"

Tobie frowned. "She's not experiencing any symptoms that I can see. If you inspected your apartment again could you tell if anything were missing?"

"Maybe."

"Tell you what, let me finish up with the patient I have

in the other exam room, then we'll go back to your apartment and see if you can tell if anything is missing. How does that sound?''

"I suppose." He pursed his lips in a dubious expression. "Do you think we'll have to pump her stomach?''

"I doubt it, but let's wait and see. I've got to check on my other patient but then I'll be right back. Call for me immediately if Molly starts having trouble. Just push this red button here." Tobie pointed to the red emergency button mounted on the wall. Briefly, she touched Clay's arm and felt his skin ripple beneath her fingers.

She glanced at Molly. The child was busy playing with her toes. She seemed happy. Clay, on the other hand, looked as if he'd been beaten up. His shoulders sagged visibly as he sat down hard on the stool.

"I'll have Lilly bring you a cup of coffee."

"Thanks."

Tobie left the room, shutting the door closed behind her. Her heart fluttered, from the excitement over Molly or the pressure of seeing Clay again, she wasn't sure which. Probably a little of both.

By the time she finished with the patient in exam room one and returned to Clay and Molly, Tobie had convinced herself the odd physical manifestation she had experienced in the hallway when she'd touched Clay was due to lack of sleep and nothing else. Exhaustion could do strange things to the human body.

"How's she doing?" Tobie asked.

Clay held Molly on his knee. The baby gurgled.

"She's fine," he replied. "Me? I need a muscle relaxer or a good stiff drink. Man, I never knew having kids could be so taxing."

"Come on," she said. "Let's make a quick run to your apartment and see if you can find what she might have swallowed."

Tobie whirled around and headed for the door. On her way out, she stopped and looked over her shoulder. The sight of Clay perched on the stool, Molly cuddled in his lap, brought a knot of emotion to her throat. Would she ever have a family of her own?

Not if you stay with Edward. The thought formed in her mind with the shocking clarity of an icy winter stream and she knew she had to break off their engagement.

Clay, with Molly in his arms, led the way into his apartment. He watched Tobie's gaze sweep the cluttered room. Her violet aroma teased his nostrils. Her hair, glossy as a raven's wing, brushed against her cheek and stirred a sensuous warmness within him. Her skin was delicate and pale as fragile porcelain. He fought a fierce urge to run his fingers along her jawline, to cup her chin in his palm, turn her face up to his and kiss those sweet pink lips.

Forget it, Barton, he told himself, she's engaged to a prominent physician. What in hades would Tobie Avery want with a mad inventor like you?

Of course if she knew his true identity, she might be more likely to go out with him. But who wanted a woman who was only after money and status? He'd begun his masquerade as a poor man in order to escape such gold diggers. No, if Tobie Avery were attracted to him, she had to be attracted to a poor man. Then, once he knew she wanted him for himself and for that reason alone, he'd reveal the truth to her.

To heck with a relationship, how about a long, sensuous night, thrashing around in his bed instead? his baser instincts argued.

Tobie walked around the sofa, eyeing the mess. Molly's walker lay on its side where it had fallen amidst the various pieces of wood, metal, wires and rubber.

Clay glanced at Tobie's long, tapered fingers resting on

her hips. She kept her fingernails filed short and buffed but wore no polish. Her hands were bare he noted, then did a double take. That horse-choking diamond was missing from her left ring finger.

"Where's your engagement ring?" he blurted out.

"I'm no longer wearing it," she replied.

"What?" His heart lightened at her words.

He could tell she was purposefully avoiding his gaze. "I'd rather not discuss my personal life, if you don't mind."

"You're ditching the doc? How come?"

"It's none of your business."

"Does it have anything to do with me?"

"Don't flatter yourself. I don't have time for this. I've got an office full of patients waiting on me." Tobie kept her eyes glued to the floor. "Now where was Molly when you found her?"

"Over here."

Tobie's heart thundered as Clay moved toward her, Molly clutched in his arms. He righted the downed walker with one hand, then waved at the work bench jam-packed with foreign objects. Any one of those dangerous looking things could be detrimental to a young child's health.

"Look it over carefully," she instructed him. "Think. Is anything missing?"

Clay shifted Molly to his hip, scratched his head and studied the work bench. "Nothing seems to be missing, but I couldn't say for sure."

Tobie let her gaze wander. She spotted an odd, oblong piece of machinery sitting next to the stereo. It looked like a trash compactor.

"What's that?" she asked.

Clay's face brightened immediately, and he puffed his chest out with pride. "That's the Barton Recycler. The machine that's going to revolutionize recycling."

Tobie stepped over to the appliance and lifted the lid. "How does it work?"

"You put any kind of plastic, paper, aluminum or glass you want in there and the recycler transforms it into a recyclable product. No longer will you have to separate your trash. Pop it in here, push the button and presto."

"That's amazing."

Clay launched into a detailed explanation of exactly how the transformation took place and how the end results could be sold and reused. Tobie didn't understand a bit of the technical jargon, but she did hear the unbridled enthusiasm in Clay's voice. He sounded knowledgeable and she could almost believe his project would succeed, then she remembered how her father would come home, brimming over with excitement at some new "get rich quick" scheme he'd invested in. She also recalled how not one single time had his grandiose ambitions materialized into anything tangible.

Was Clay Barton any different from her dad? Or did her attraction to him signal some deep-seated psychological problem relating back to her childhood and her unresolved conflicts with her itinerant father?

She had thought her attraction to Clay Barton might have something to do with Molly and her sudden longing to have a child. Standing next to him, she noticed his fingers were nicked with scars and stained with chemical compounds. Tobie knew the attraction ran much deeper than the fact he was good with children. She wanted to experience those rough fingers caressing her soft skin. She yearned to sip the nectar of his honeyed lips. She longed to inhale his clean, slightly metallic scent.

Face facts, Tobie Avery, you want Clay Barton's body. Don't do it, she warned herself. Don't you dare start falling for this guy. He represented everything she'd struggled her entire life to escape. He was good-looking and tender with the baby, but husband material? Most definitely not.

Molly wriggled in Clay's arms and whined. Bending over, he settled her into the walker.

"So? What do you think?"

"Huh?" Tobie blinked, startled.

"Wool gathering?"

"My mind wandered. I'm sorry. That was rude of me."

The grin he surrendered was poignant and lopsided. Why did he have to be so damned irresistible?

"What do you think of the Barton Recycler?"

"Sounds good in theory."

"Theory nothing. It's almost ready to be patented."

He stared at her, firm and steady. Mesmerized by the strength in those eyes, Tobie dropped her gaze. Confusion clouded her senses. Anxiety tensed in the pit of her stomach, coiling into a clot of sensual wariness.

She cleared her throat. "So you don't think Molly swallowed anything?"

He grimaced. "I can't say for sure."

Tobie looked at the baby grinning up at her from the walker. "She seems fine. I think she just sucked on the filament."

"I hope you're right. Now I see what they mean when they say kids will give you gray hair."

Tobie sneaked a look at Clay's head of thick, light brown hair. He would look quite distinguished gray, she decided, the color complementing his steely eyes.

Tobie stuck her hand in her pocket and closed her fist around Edward's ring. Physical desires aside, Clay wasn't the disease, but rather the symptom of her discontent. And he was definitely not the cure. She could never give herself to a man who lived in a dream world, no matter how appealing he might be. Her fascination with him, however, had shown Tobie one thing clearly. She wasn't in love with Dr. Edward Bennet and never had been. She'd been willing to marry him because she craved security. Edward represented the dependability she'd never had while growing up. Shame flared through her as the realization settled in. She had to break things off with Edward as soon as possible. She could not continue the charade of pretending to love him.

"Miss Molly Malone appears to be enjoying herself," Clay said.

"She's a lovely baby," Tobie said wistfully. That was another reason to leave Edward. If she married him, she would probably never have children of her own.

"I bet *you* were a beautiful baby."

Clay's touch was tentative and gentle. The heat from his fingers sent a tingle of expectation winging up her arm and suffusing her entire body in a warm, sparkling glow.

When he pulled her into his arms, she didn't offer even a murmur of protest. She didn't think, just sank against that broad chest and let his essence enfold her like the soft security of a down mattress. Absorbing his fire, she closed her eyes, knowing what was coming and wanting it with every fiber of her being. She'd wanted his kiss from the first moment she'd made contact with those stormy gray eyes.

Her hand curled around his cotton shirt, she could feel the corded muscle beneath her fingers. She reacted to his touch the way flowers react to the sun, reaching, hungry, searching for the warm light.

Tobie tilted her head back and waited.

Clay took her hand in his, pressed her so close she melded into his skin. His lips came down on hers, weightless as butterfly wings. That first taste of him was rich and sweet as homemade ice cream. She wanted more. More.

His lips moved, exploring. She felt as if she were leisurely floating in a pool of cool water, languid, lazy, engulfed in the experience.

Clay deepened the kiss. Time ceased. Tobie acknowledged nothing but Clay's lips and the steady throbbing of her own heart.

He placed one hand at the small of her back, caressing her skin and sending tingles to every nerve ending in her body. He searched her mouth with his tongue, and Tobie breathed in a heady sigh.

The hand at the small of her back inched up her spine until he ensnared his fingers in her hair.

She returned the kiss with increasing intensity. She heard Molly coo, but her mind didn't register the sound. It seemed as if Clay had stolen all her senses and bottled them up inside him.

A deep, throaty groan exploded from his throat as he broke the kiss and buried his face in the curve of her neck. His tongue licked flames down her throat until Tobie wriggled with desire. So many sensations rioted in her body she couldn't identify them all. Her breasts felt heavy, anxious, eager to share in the pleasure.

"Oh, Tobie," he moaned, bringing a hand to caress her breast as if he knew exactly what she needed. "I want to make love to you."

His words jerked her eyes open as she realized what they were doing. If they didn't stop now, she couldn't be held responsible for her actions.

"This is wrong," she said, placing her hands on his chest and pushing away. "I haven't told Edward the engagement is off."

"Tell him. Soon," Clay rasped. "You can't love him if you can kiss me like that."

Confused, Tobie turned away, brought a hand to her throbbing mouth. "I have to be going," she gasped. "Call me if Molly shows any symptoms."

"Tobie, wait." He reached out to her, but she spun away. Unable to deal with her feelings, she wanted nothing more than to get as far from Clay Barton as possible.

"I have to go. I have patients."

Without another look back, without another word, Tobie turned and fled.

Clay watched her leave, his heart settling into his stomach. He couldn't deny the powerful feelings she stirred in him. After that dynamic kiss, he knew he had to have her. There must be some way to convince Tobie to give him a chance.

"Oooo," Molly cooed.

Gazing down at the baby, an idea began to hatch in Clay's mind. He stroked his chin with a thumb and index finger. Hmm. Babies seemed to be Dr. Avery's weakness. What if he could persuade her to help him out with Molly? What if he played on her sympathies, gave her the "I'm just a poor, inept bachelor" speech? What if he made it sound as if Molly would suffer without her help? Actually that might not be so far from the truth if the last two days' adventures were any indication. Of course Tobie need never know he could afford to hire a nanny. He knew if he could just spend more time with Tobie something very interesting might develop between them. Yes. That was the answer, get Tobie to feel sorry for him and Molly.

"Barton," Clay said out loud. "You're a genius."

Chapter Four

Nervously Tobie fidgeted as she drove through the winding, security patrolled streets of the exclusive West Over Hills neighborhood. Most of the stately manors ringing the road were protected by iron fences and dense, well-tended foliage, giving the impression of countryside privacy even though downtown Fort Worth lay only a few miles east. Expensive vehicles graced long driveways. Most houses boasted swimming pools. Some even claimed their own tennis courts. Many had been featured in luxurious-living magazines. The residents were bankers and pilots, doctors and lawyers. Their children went to private schools; their clothes were tailor-made. No get-rich-quick schemers or eccentric inventors could be found in this affluent community.

Someday, Tobie hoped to live here, too. When she finally had her struggling medical practice on an even keel, when she paid off those numerous school loans. Five or ten years from now she would join the affluent ranks. Until then she saved every spare penny toward her ultimate goal—lifelong security.

From the time she was a small child, Tobie had fallen asleep on cheap mattresses, her stomach grumbling hungrily, while visions of the perfect husband, a lovely mansion and expensive furniture waltzed in her head. She dreamed of gourmet food and designer clothing. She'd fantasized about hobnobbing with the rich and famous. Then Edward had come into her life, with promises that captured her childish fantasies. But now she was a grown woman, ready to relinquish the old goals that had fortified her through her formative years and start afresh with new hopes and dreams more suited to her adult status. Dreams that stretched beyond material belongings. Dreams that included children and true love.

She toyed with the faux pearl necklace at her throat, twisting the smooth beads between her fingers. Edward had invited her to help him host a small dinner party, although his definition of *small* meant ten couples. Like most everyone else in West Over Hills, Dr. Edward Bennet entertained on a grand scale. Tobie had decided this was the opportunity she needed to tell Edward their relationship was over. After the guests left, she intended to give him back his ring and car and take a taxi home.

Ending the engagement was not going to be easy. Over and over, she'd rehearsed the words in her head, but nothing sounded right. Wryly, she thought of the Paul Simon tune, "Fifty Ways to Leave Your Lover." In her mind she could hear Paul's voice saying "Just get yourself free." Gee, where was Mr. Simon when you needed him?

In her clutch purse, the same sapphire blue as her silk dress, lay Edward's ring. The day he'd given it to her, she'd been excited and proud, but she hadn't felt the unrestrained happiness she should have experienced. Looking back, Tobie had known when she'd accepted the ring that she hadn't loved Edward. Was her hunger for guaranteed security so great she'd been willing to sell herself short? Apparently so. If nothing else, she had Clay Barton to thank for forcing her to open her eyes and take a good look at herself.

Clay Barton. Helplessly, irresistibly, Tobie's thoughts were drawn to the young inventor and his charming little niece. Why couldn't she stop thinking about that man? He'd been eating at her thoughts for the past two days, and for the life of her, she could not say why. So he was good-looking. Big deal. Lanky, handsome, untamed types were as common as street lamps. Why Clay? Why now?

For years, she'd often repeated the adage "It's as easy to fall in love with a rich man as a poor one." But now she wondered if that were true. Could one really control love? Because of her difficult childhood, she'd longed for the stability and security that money could bring, but in her heart it wasn't possessions she craved. Instead, she simply wanted the assurance that she'd never be reduced to sleeping in a tent or digging food from garbage cans as her family had done on occasions.

Old fears died hard. She was a physician now; she could provide for herself. Yet she could not shake the underlying terror that some tragedy would strike and she would lose it all.

Tobie took a deep breath and turned down the block that led to Edward's house. She passed a sprawling plantation-style estate on her right and a dignified Tudor on her left. The Tudor appealed to her senses. She liked the safe, homey image the ivy-covered walls evoked. The architecture was the antithesis to Edward's modernist palace perched on the hill just ahead. His house had always struck her as cold and austere with its sleek lines and sharp angles.

Stopping at the security gate, Tobie rolled down the window and punched in the access code. The metal doors slid open and she went through, her heart hammering.

A valet was waiting for her as she drove up. Putting the

car into park, she grabbed her clutch purse and relinquished the vehicle to the tuxedoed attendant.

Edward greeted her at the door, dressed impeccably as always. He kissed her lightly on the cheek, then led her inside.

"You look ravishing," he murmured.

"Thank you." Tobie cleared her throat, suddenly feeling very awkward.

"That color of blue becomes you," he said, linking his arm through hers and guiding her into the living room.

"Thank you."

A full bar had been set up with a bartender at the ready, a pristine white towel draped over one of his arms. Classical music, tinkling and inoffensive, sifted in through the elaborate speaker system piped into the walls.

"Would you like something to drink?" Edward offered.

"Mineral water," she told the mustachioed bartender.

"No wine tonight, darling?" Edward arched an eyebrow.

Tobie shook her head. When she broke things off with Edward, she wanted perfect control over her senses.

Taking the water the bartender offered, she turned to sit down on the white leather sofa. Although she'd seen Edward's house before, tonight Tobie surveyed her surroundings with fresh eyes. Except for the splash of color from the modern art hanging under track lighting, the entire room was done in black, white and silver. Black overstuffed leather chairs, thick white carpeting, a glistening chrome coffee table and floor lamp. The overall effect was sterile, cold, passionless.

Tobie thought of Clay Barton and his messy apartment. She remembered the scraggly moose head on the wall and suppressed a smile. What would Clay think of Edward's home?

"Something amusing?" Edward asked, settling himself in on the sofa beside her.

"What time are you expecting the guests?" she asked, avoiding his question.

He glanced at the expensive watch nestled at his wrist. "Seven-thirty. We have an hour. I wanted to discuss something with you before they arrive."

"Edward, there's something I need to discuss with you, as well, but I think it should keep until after the party."

"As you wish."

"What's your news?" She fidgeted with her purse clasp.

A triumphant grin crossed his face. "I'm announcing my candidacy for president of the AMA. I've got the complete backing of Dr. Kemper and his bunch. There's no telling how far I can go. Today president of the AMA, tomorrow surgeon general."

"I'm pleased for you."

"You could show a little more enthusiasm," Edward chided. "How would you like to be the first lady of medicine, my dear?"

"I'd rather be a mom," she blurted out.

He gave her an annoyed glance. "We've been through this before, Tobie. I thought we had an understanding."

"Things have changed. I've been having maternal yearnings lately." She hadn't meant to tell him yet. She'd planned to wait until after the party when they could be alone. Darting a glance at the bartender, Tobie lowered her voice, clenched her hands.

"After Millicent died I raised our three children alone. I'm forty-five years old and in the prime of my life, I can't be saddled with babies at this point."

"I'm happy for you, Edward, truly. I know becoming president of the AMA is a long-held goal for you."

"It's for you too, honey. Think about all the extra things I'll be able to give you. A bigger house, a nicer car, beautiful clothes. We'll travel, meet interesting new friends, dine at exotic restaurants. All the things you never had."

A week ago the scenario Edward painted still might have appealed to her, but since Clay Barton and his niece Molly had come charging into her life, Tobie found her needs had changed. Stability was still important, yes, but now she longed for more. She wanted children as well!

Why wait until the end of the night to sever their engagement? She knew she had no future with Edward. Why prolong things? Swallowing hard, Tobie opened her clutch purse and extracted his ring, the large diamond winking in the light. She regretted having to hurt Edward, but she simply could not continue their association. Her strong physical reaction to Clay Barton told her that much.

"I want to return this." She extended the ring in her open palm.

"Tobie? What are you trying to say to me?"

Lacing her fingers together, Tobie stared at her lap. She couldn't bear to see the pain reflected in Edward's eyes, knowing she was responsible for his suffering.

"Tobie, look at me."

She lifted her chin and met his gaze. He was a handsome man who had not softened in middle age, and his gray hair only served to accentuate his distinguished air. His perfect posture announced to the world at large that Dr. Edward Bennet was a man to be reckoned with. In fact, it was his steady, rock-solid appearance that had attracted Tobie to him in the first place. But when she looked into his eyes her heart did not race, nor did her palms sweat. She did not feel giddy or tongue-tied or breathless.

"What is the meaning of this?" He took the ring from her, folded it in his hands.

"I can't marry you."

"Why not? What's happened?"

Tobie squirmed in her chair. She felt nauseous.

"You've met someone else, haven't you?" he accused, a frown furrowing his elegant brow.

"No," Tobie said. The image of bare chested Clay Barton, clutching baby Molly in his arms popped unbidden into her mind. She shook her head. "No," she repeated again, as much for herself as for Edward's benefit. This decision was not based on her inexplicable attraction to Clay Barton. In all probability she'd never see the man again. This issue was strictly between her and Edward.

"It's that man isn't it?" Edward sounded positively jealous. He leaned forward and fixed her to the spot with an icy glare. "The one who had the sick baby the night you made that house call."

The uncanny accuracy of Edward's assessment sent a shiver through her. Had he somehow sensed her attraction to Clay? But that was silly. He had no way of knowing about her unruly desire for the eccentric inventor.

"You don't mean Clay Barton?" Tobie replied hotly. "For goodness sakes, don't be ridiculous. His child was my patient. That's all."

"Clay Barton." Edward's frown deepened; he drummed his fingers on the coffee table. "Where have I heard that name before? Is he related to Carlton Barton, the oil and gas magnate?"

Clay? Kin to one of the richest men in Fort Worth? That was a laugh. "I seriously doubt it."

"Then you haven't found another man?"

"Not at all," she denied coolly. "I just want children."

"I'm not willing to supply them."

"I know. That's why I'm setting you free. You never needed me anyway."

"That's not true," he protested. "I do need you."

"You'll find someone else. You have a lot to offer the right woman."

He took her hand in his. "Tobie, I care about you very much."

"I care about you, too, Edward, but caring isn't enough. I want Fourth of July fireworks."

They sat staring at each other. Tobie was fully aware Edward had never uttered the word *love*. She untangled her hand from his and got to her feet. "I think I better be going."

"What am I suppose to tell my guests?" he asked at last.

"Tell them anything you want. Say you broke the engagement. It doesn't matter."

Was that all he cared about? What his friends would think? Edward appeared surprisingly unruffled, his face devoid of emotions. No one would take him for a man who had just been dumped by his fiancée. If Clay Barton were here and she was breaking off *their* engagement, she knew without a doubt he would not be so nonchalant. The kiss he had bestowed upon her told Tobie that much. No, if Clay was in Edward's shoes he would definitely be passionate, he might shout or demand an explanation or slam his fist on the table but he most certainly would not take rejection with undisturbed equanimity. What she'd once mistaken in Edward for steadfast coolness was instead indifference.

"What about all the arrangements? The gifts?" he asked.

"I'll cancel everything. Send the presents back. Don't worry."

"What about tonight's party?"

"I was always lousy at entertaining and you know it," she said.

"I don't know what to say."

"The valet has the keys to your car. Under the circumstances I can not keep it." She opened and closed her purse clasp repeatedly.

He stared at her, and for a split second Tobie thought he

was going to argue. Then he shrugged. "If that's the way you really want it."

"Could you please call me a cab?" Tobie asked the bartender. The man nodded and picked up the phone.

"I can't believe you'd walk out on me like this," Edward complained. "Something has happened to you. You've never been so thoughtless before."

How like Edward. To assume this was a plot to ruin his evening. He was put out because she was spoiling his party. That was it? A year of her life wasted on Dr. Edward Bennet and he wasn't even going to acknowledge the commitment they'd shared?

"I'm sorry," she said. At that moment she felt like crying. Her bottom lip quivered.

"Hey." Edward squeezed her arm. "It's not the end of the world. We'll both survive. I need someone to back me up in my career, and you need a man to give you babies. Good thing we figured that out before we got married."

"Yes."

"Well, I suppose there's nothing left to say. If this is what you really want, I won't stand in your way."

"Thank you."

Edward bowed, inclined his head in a brief nod.

"If you don't mind, I prefer to wait for the cab outside," Tobie said.

"As you wish."

The minute the front door closed behind her she felt as if a giant stone had been lifted from her chest. Free. She was a single woman again, and the next time she got engaged she wanted not only a stable, dependable man but one who adored babies, as well!

"Well Miss Molly Malone, are you happy now?" Clay looked over at his niece strapped into the car seat beside him. He'd spent the afternoon getting the car running again so he could make a trip across town to Anne's place in West Over Hills simply to retrieve Molly's special blanket.

After talking to his sister on the phone that afternoon, they'd finally identified the source of her frequent crying jags. The kid liked to sleep with a special blanket, and in her frenzied state, Anne had forgotten to tell Clay about Molly's bedtime preference.

The streetlights came on against the descending twilight. Molly sucked her thumb while resting her head on the blanket. She looked so darned cute Clay wished he had a camera to capture the moment. Wait until Tobie found out about the cause of Molly's distress.

At the thought of Tobie Avery, Clay blew out his breath. So far his campaign to get her to help him out with Molly had been a bust. When he'd called her earlier that afternoon to invite her out to dinner, Lilly had told him Tobie had left to get ready for a party with her fiancé. That's when Clay realized how foolish he was lusting, after an engaged woman.

"Just forget about Tobie," Clay spoke out loud. "You've got other things to worry about." Like taking care of Molly and finishing the work on his recycler. "Obviously it wasn't meant to be between us."

As soon as he muttered the words, Clay saw her. Dr. Tobie Avery appeared out of nowhere, standing on the street corner looking forlorn and uncomfortable in a beautiful blue silk dress. It was as if he'd conjured her up out of the ether, a fairy-tale princess just waiting to be rescued.

Clay slammed on the brakes.

His heart stuttered in his chest like a misfiring engine. She looked startled to see him, her blue eyes widening in surprise. Oh, damn. He needed an excuse for being in West Over Hills. He'd never convince Tobie to move in with him for a few days and help out with Molly if she knew he was wealthy enough to afford a nanny. And now that he'd seen her again, Clay knew he would not abandon his crusade to maneuver Dr. Avery into his bed. He needed a plausible story, fast.

Rolling down the window, Clay leaned out. "Hey, gorgeous, need a ride? Barton Limousine Service at your command."

Was it his imagination or was she very happy to see him? A big grin splashed across her face. She scurried around to the passenger side door and wrenched it open. The aging door creaked a protest.

"Thanks a million. I've been waiting thirty minutes for a cab."

"Let me put Molly in the back," Clay offered. Quickly he transferred the baby and the car seat into the back, then put the car in gear.

"What are you doing in West Over Hills?" Tobie asked, buckling her seat belt.

Think, Barton, think. When in doubt, take the offensive.

"What? Aren't I good enough to drive around this hoity-toity neighborhood?"

To his surprise, Tobie blushed. "Of course you're good enough. This just doesn't seem like your type of place, that's all."

He wondered what she would say if she knew his sister owned the Tudor home down the block.

"For your information, I came here for some child-rearing advice." That much was true. While at Anne's house, he'd talked to her maid about Molly. "A friend of mine is a live-in maid for some rich folks. I told you I was a poor bachelor who knew nothing about raising babies. Since you wouldn't take pity on me, I had to seek help elsewhere."

What was *she* doing in West Over Hills, he pondered. Did her fiancé live here? Was Tobie another gold digger? Until he trusted her, Clay knew he could never reveal his

true identity. She certainly looked stunning in that silk
sheath. The clingy material accentuated her smooth curves,
the color enhanced her blue eyes. She could have any man
she wanted, rich, poor or in between.

"Where's your car?" he asked.

"I no longer own the sports car."

"Oh?"

"I gave it back to Edward."

His grin widened, his heart suddenly light. "Does that
mean your engagement is off?"

"He doesn't want children," she said, by way of explanation.

"Foolish man."

"I agree."

Molly muttered gibberish as if putting in her two-cents
worth. Tobie and Clay laughed in response.

"How do you plan on getting back and forth to work?"
Clay asked.

"I suppose I'll rent a vehicle."

"That can get expensive. I just got this jalopy running
again."

"I'm glad you've got transportation," she said. "You
need it with a baby in the house. This weekend I plan to
go car shopping."

"Hey, I could go with you. I'm pretty good at wheeling
and dealing car salesmen."

"I appreciate the offer, but I don't want to be a bother."

"I've got an even better idea. Why don't you stay with
Molly and me for a few days."

Tobie frowned and folded her arms across her chest as
if protecting herself. "I don't think so."

"Why not? It makes perfect sense." He saw denial war
with acquiescence on her face. She wanted to say yes! He
could tell by the spark in her eyes. If he pressed, she'd
cave. "Come on, Tobie, it'd save you a bundle in car rental

fees and cab fare. If you're buying a new car you'll need
the money for a down payment."

"I wouldn't want to impose."

Tobie an imposition? Not likely. "Where do you live?"
Clay asked, leaving West Over Hills and guiding the car
onto the highway.

"Candleridge."

"On the other side of Hulen?"

"Yes."

"That's a long way."

"You can take me to your apartment, and I'll call a cab
from there."

"Why don't you stay with us tonight?" he tried again.
"You're more than welcome. And I do need help with
Molly. I haven't even fed her supper yet."

"I can't go to work tomorrow dressed like this." She
frowned and spread a hand at her lavish gown.

Clay conceded the point. Dang but she was a tough nut
to crack. In his entire life he'd never met a female so im-
mune to him. Of course, before he'd become a social hermit, the women had been lining up at his front door. He
had never had to go looking. Actually it bruised his ego a
bit to realize Dr. Tobie Avery did not find him irresistible.

"Come on, I don't mind driving you home and waiting
for you to pack a few things."

"Oh, no, I couldn't ask you to go out of your way like
that."

"Why not? What else have Molly and I got to do?"

"I thought you were working on the Barton Recycler."

Clay shrugged. "It'll keep. Truthfully, you'd be doing
me a favor. I need a break and adult conversation. Molly
isn't exactly facile in the English language." Tobie hesitated, and Clay knew he had her.

"Well?" he asked. "What do you say? You helped me
with Molly in my hour of need, let me return the favor."

Molly grunted from the back seat, and Tobie turned around to check on her. Clay noticed the tender, wistful way she gazed at the baby. Why did he want so badly to convince her to stay with him? What was it about Tobie Avery that pushed all the right buttons inside him? Was it her sweet violet aroma or her long shapely legs or her silky black hair that lit his fire? Was it the potent combination of all three physical characteristics plus her loyal, caring nature?

The only thing Clay knew for sure, Tobie Avery excited him like no woman before. Simply thinking about her produced a rich heaviness in his groin that made him yearn to scoop her into his arms, drag her off like a caveman and make love to her all night long.

His eyes searched her face, explored her delicate skin, her expressive blue eyes. He remembered the succulent taste of her lips and almost groaned in response.

Clay Barton had a plan designed to thaw the ice princess. If he could manage to chisel past the glacier guarding her heart, Tobie would surrender to him like Snow White awakening to her lover's kiss.

And the little dynamo in the car seat behind them was the key to Tobie Avery's undoing.

Why not stay at Clay's? Tobie thought. It would certainly simplify things. His apartment was only two blocks from the office and besides, she didn't relish spending the night alone. And of course that didn't mean anything had to develop between them. She'd make that clear from the very start. After all, Clay had pleaded with her in the most charming way and she believed he sincerely thought he needed her help with Molly.

A warm sensation seeped through her. She was glad to see Clay and Molly again. From the time he'd pulled his jalopy to a halt outside Edward's house, she couldn't stop admiring how handsome he looked in that leather jacket with the collar turned up. His clean, tangy scent teased her nostrils. The lurch of awareness invading her body staggered Tobie with its intensity.

She finger combed her hair and bit down on her lips to redden them, then realized what she was doing. Good grief! She was trying to make herself more attractive for Clay Barton. Had she lost her mind? She had to stop thinking like this. Nothing could come of her attraction to this scrumptious inventor. He had been the catalyst for getting her out of her relationship with Edward and nothing more. She had best remember that.

"All right," she said.

"Excuse me?"

"I'll stay the night at your place, but only under one condition."

"Yes?" He guided the sedan into his apartment complex. Parking beneath a security light, he cut the engine.

"I will not have a repeat performance of what happened this morning in your apartment."

"What do you mean?" he asked, feigning innocence.

"No more kissing."

"Ah, shucks, you're no fun," he teased.

"I'm serious, Clay. I just broke up with my fiancé and I'm very vulnerable. The last thing I'm interested in is a rebound relationship. I'll accept your hospitality and spend the night here because it's convenient and you need help with Molly. Obviously I can't ignore a child in need. But that's it. Understood?"

He saluted her. "Yes, ma'am."

She unbuckled her seat belt and slid out of the car. Waiting patiently on the sidewalk while Clay removed Molly from the car seat and tucked a pink blanket around her, Tobie struggled to explain the attraction she had for this man.

Clay Barton represented everything she did not want in a life partner. He was a dreamer with no real ambitions. Kindhearted yes, but too undisciplined for his own good. He reminded her so much of her father. But despite his faults, he roused something in her. A feeling she'd never experienced before and was too frightened to name.

Following him up the steps, her eyes trained on his cocky swagger, a sensation of dread settled over her. By staying here, she was tempting fate, waving a red flag in the face of destiny. Tobie gulped. Had she just made the biggest mistake of her life?

Chapter Five

Stepping over the threshold into Clay's apartment, Tobie immediately noticed he'd cleaned the place up since her visit earlier that afternoon. The various mechanical parts that had been strewn across the room were neatly shelved in clear plastic containers and lined along the top of the bookcase safely out of harm's reach. The floor had been vacuumed free of debris. Obviously, he'd taken the scare with Molly very seriously.

"Have a seat," he offered, "while I go start supper."

"Can I help?" she asked.

He sent an appreciative gaze over her body, his eyes lingering at her curves. "I don't think you're dressed for kitchen duty."

"Well at least let me hold Molly."

"Sure."

She held out her hands, and Molly was transferred from Clay's hip to Tobie's.

Clay wandered into the kitchen, flipping on lights as he went. "I was planning on broiled chicken breasts and mashed potatoes, how does that sound?"

"Don't go to any extra trouble on my account," Tobie said, trailing behind him.

"Hey, I'm ready for a home cooked meal. Most of my dinners come from a box."

"So do mine," Tobie confessed. "Or I usually eat supper at Edward's functions. Guess I won't be doing that anymore." Molly chewed on her own hand, a string of drool dripped from her chin. Tobie retrieved a paper towel from the rack and dabbed at the baby's chin. "Molly's teething," she observed. "Do you have any teething biscuits?"

Clay nodded his head in the direction of the pantry. "Help yourself." He rolled up his sleeves, revealing forearms that would put any cattle wrangler to shame and began peeling potatoes in the sink.

While Clay worked, Tobie pulled out a chair at the kitchen table and sat down with Molly in her lap, the baby happily chewing on her teething biscuit.

"Are you going to miss your old life-style?" Clay asked suddenly, a dark, unreadable look clouding his eyes.

Tobie looked up. "What do you mean?"

"The fancy parties, the gourmet food, the excitement you must have become accustomed to."

"Are you kidding?" Tobie wrinkled her nose. "After a year of banquet food, home cooking is pure heaven."

Clay looked relieved. "You really won't miss all the things your fiancé could have given you?"

Tobie shrugged. Was Clay fishing to see how she'd feel about dating a poor man? The thought deserved consideration. Sure she'd wanted a nice house and the stable life Edward could offer, but over the past two days she'd come to realize neither of those things was worth a loveless, childless existence.

But on the flip side, could she enter into a loving marriage that promised absolutely no dependability? Could she mate with a man who couldn't provide for his family? She remembered those awful days following her father's death when she and her mother had been evicted. The memories hurt even now—food stamps, welfare, the stark fear of never knowing if they would have enough food to eat or a warm, dry place to sleep.

"Tobie?"

"What?" She blinked, pulled from her reverie by Clay's voice.

"You looked so serious," he said lightly. "What were you thinking?"

"Nothing," Tobie denied, unprepared to share her innermost thoughts with him. Communicating on that level produced intimacy, and under the circumstances she needed to keep as much distance between them as possible. Falling into close familiarity with Clay Barton would be far too easy.

Molly squirmed in her lap, providing a much-needed diversion. She settled the little girl to the floor. The atmosphere in the kitchen was nice, homey. She and Clay were like new parents, sharing the responsibility of preparing supper and child care. Wistfulness filled her. Would she ever have a home, a family of her own?

"Let me help," she said, hoping to dispel such thoughts through action. Grabbing a pot holder from the counter, she opened the oven door, pulled out the broiler rack and turned the chicken. Whirling around, fork in hand, she almost ran smack dab into Clay's broad chest.

"Hold on there." He reached out a hand to steady her.

"Oh," she said breathlessly as his arm reached around her waist.

"You okay?"

"Fine," she whispered. "A little dizzy I guess, from bending over the hot oven."

Every time she gazed at Clay Barton, she felt the same

light-headed swooning sensation that had nothing to do with bending or hot ovens. He was standing so close she could see those long eyelashes framing his lively gray eyes. A lopsided smile crooked the corner of his mouth.

"Where's Molly," she asked.

They both looked around and spotted the baby prying open a cabinet door.

"No, no," Clay scolded. He firmly shut the cabinet. Molly pouched out her bottom lip and crawled under the kitchen table.

Clay shook his head. "I've got to get baby latches installed on these cabinets. She sure scared the stuffing out of me today, gnawing on that iron filament. I'm so glad you were there for us."

"My pleasure."

As if she knew they were discussing her, Molly plopped down on her diapered bottom, clapped her hands together and cooed.

They chuckled in unison at the darling picture Molly made. Inexplicably, Tobie's gaze was drawn once more to Clay's. Laughter had widened his smile, Tobie couldn't help grinning in response. It felt so good, so right, to be in this apartment with these two. She'd almost forgotten the circumstances that had landed her here.

"Supper's nearly ready," Clay announced.

Tobie nodded, and for a magical second everything seemed to recede to a faraway level, the food on the stove, the baby under the table, the whole rest of the apartment. Suddenly, it was just the two of them on a secret planet of their own. She sucked in her breath, let her gaze linger on Clay's features. His strong nose, his capable chin, his steady clear-eyed gaze. Her gaze trailed lower to his mouth, and she remembered sharply, poignantly, the tantalizing taste of him. How could she ever have perceived this man as unreliable?

Stop it, Tobie Lynne Avery, she scolded. You're letting your fantasies run away with your common sense. Stop turning Clay Barton into something he's not. Just because you're attracted to him, don't attribute him with qualities he does not possess.

Molly squealed and crawled out from under the table. The baby's little palms patted against the linoleum as she headed straight for Clay's legs. Bending down, he retrieved Molly and swung her onto his hip.

With shaky hands, Tobie brushed a lock of hair from her eyes and turned away. What was this strange fascination Clay Barton aroused within her? How could she possibly combat his tempting allure while residing in his home?

Keep way from him, her prudent side urged. Use Molly as a buffer, then get the heck out of here, ASAP.

"Wanna check on the potatoes for me?" Clay asked, struggling to keep a secure grip on the wriggling baby.

"Sure." Tobie lifted the pan lid and poked a fork in the potatoes. Satisfied they were done, she drained the spuds in a strainer and dumped them into a bowl, then added margarine and milk.

Clay leaned against the counter, watching her. She was definitely independent. And proud. The haughty tilt to her head spoke volumes. He sensed she would resent any interference on his part. Idly he wondered what childhood environment had produced these staunch characteristics in her.

Damn, but she captivated him. From her pristine Snow White beauty to her lithe, graceful movements, she'd set up residence in his mind, and no matter how hard he tried, Clay couldn't seem to evict her. He wanted her. Plain and simple. Or maybe ornate and complicated, because the last thing he needed at this point in his life was a long-term commitment. He ached for her, and he was unsure how much of himself he could give at this point. His inventions meant everything to him, how would marriage and a family fit in with his career choice? But what harm could a temporary romantic interlude do?

Except something told him Dr. Tobie Avery was not the temporary type. Then, too, there was the matter of her broken engagement. Had she ended her association with her fiancé because of that kiss they'd shared?

Don't be an egotistical swine, Barton. You're not that great a kisser. Still, he couldn't help but wonder. It was great having her here to help him with Molly, and he thanked his lucky stars she'd agreed to stay the night.

While Tobie set the food on the table, Clay settled Molly into her high chair. The baby jabbered away like a miniature queen holding court.

He opened two jars of baby food. One pureed chicken, the other green beans. Pouring them into a plastic dish, he added a plop of mashed potatoes to the ensemble.

"May I feed her?" Tobie asked.

"Sure." Clay handed her the plate. He straddled the chair on Molly's left while Tobie seated herself on the right.

At the sight of her dinner, Molly opened her mouth wide and made sucking noises.

"Are you hungry, sweetheart?" Tobie murmured, scooping up a spoonful of vegetables and feeding the child. "You like that? Yes. Num-num, good."

The sound of Tobie's light, pellucid tones sent a shaft of longing straight through Clay's heart. Until this moment he had not realized how much he wanted a wife and baby of his own.

Not now, Barton. Not until he'd patented the recycler. By then he'd be ready to reveal his true identity to Tobie. But first he had to make sure she would value him for himself and not his money.

"Look, Clay," Tobie laughed as Molly reached for the spoon. "She wants to feed herself."

"Let her have at it."

"She'll make a mess."

"So. She's washable."

Tobie relinquished the spoon, and Molly stirred it around on her plate, slinging green bean mush across the high chair tray. She favored them with a green-faced smile and squeezed mashed potatoes between her fingers.

"She's so cute." Tobie giggled. "I never realized how much fun babies could be."

"Eat while she's distracted," Clay suggested, indicating Tobie's plate with his knife. "Once she loses interest, all is lost."

Following Clay's advice, Tobie dug into her meal, surprised at her hearty appetite. Lately, she'd been uninterested in eating, but the events of the day had whetted her appetite. Everything tasted so delicious, she felt as if she were savoring food for the first time in her life. The potatoes were creamy, the salad crisp, the chicken juicy and succulent.

She looked up to catch Clay watching her. An unexpected warmth suffused her system. A warmness that had everything to do with the lanky, broad-shouldered man sitting across from her. What was it about Clay Barton that made her temperature soar?

A wayward lock of hair flopped across his forehead. She itched to reach over and brush it back into place, but the thought of touching him sent shivers skipping through her body. Looking at him was bad enough. When he smiled, she found herself thinking of heated tropical breezes, ocean waves crashing against breakers and long embraces on sandy beaches. Lord, what the man could do to her with one glance.

To break the power of his gray-eyed gaze, Tobie averted

her attention to the baby. Molly was busily finger-painting with her supper, paying absolutely no heed to the adults.

The firm muscles in Clay's forearm flexed as he sliced off a piece of chicken and forked a bite into his mouth. The provocative sight of his pink tongue almost proved to be her undoing. She had no idea simply dining with a man could be so erotic.

As they were finishing dinner, the phone rang. Clay pushed back from the table, and Tobie breathed a sigh of relief. One more minute and she feared she might throw him to the kitchen floor and force herself on him. Did she dare to spend the night here?

"Hello?"

Tobie stood and began clearing the table.

"Anne! How are you? How's your mother-in-law?"

She tried not to eavesdrop, but it was a small kitchen.

"Molly's fine. Don't worry about her." Clay cradled the receiver against his chin and shoulder.

Rinsing the dishes in the sink, Tobie began loading the dishwasher.

"No. No I didn't." She noticed how Clay cast an uneasy glance in her direction. Was he embarrassed having her in his apartment? His next comment dispelled that notion.

"I have a friend staying here to help me with Molly. No, you don't know her."

Clay turned his back to Tobie and leaned against the wall, gifting her with a superb view of his well-formed backside. She gulped against the flame of desire that raced through her solar plexus at the bewitching sight.

"She's a doctor. Yes. Sure. Take your time." Clay was quiet for a moment, and from what Tobie could ascertain from the one-way conversation, his sister was giving him detailed instruction on Molly's care.

"Bye-bye, you take care. We'll see you next week, then."

Clay hung up and turned around to face Tobie. "That was my sister," he explained.

Tobie nodded. "I figured as much."

"It's still touch and go with her mother-in-law."

"I'm sorry to hear that."

"So Miss Molly Malone is with me at least another four or five days."

As if on cue, Molly opened her mouth and squalled. She had mashed potatoes plastered in her hair and pureed chicken ground into her clothes. Food dripped from the high chair, splattered to the floor. Clay looked at Tobie.

"You want the high chair or the kid?" he asked.

"The kid." Tobie stepped over and released Molly from her prison. The baby was truly sobbing now, fat tears rolling down her chubby cheeks. "Now, now, no need to get upset. We'll have you clean in a jiffy."

"Watch your clothes," Clay warned, but it was too late. Molly reached out and wrapped her arms around Tobie's neck.

Her evening gown was ruined, plastered with food, but Tobie didn't mind. She loved the feeling of the sweet baby glued to her body. Molly buried her face in the curve of Tobie's shoulder and instantly stopped crying.

"Come on, Miss Mess, let's get you cleaned up."

"I'll help," Clay volunteered. "I've bathed her by myself, I know how difficult the task can become. I'll deal with the high chair later, while you shower."

Clay was right. She *was* going to have to shower.

Carrying Molly into the bathroom, she stood looking into the mirror and making funny faces at the baby while Clay filled the tub with tepid water, then stepped to the small apartment-sized clothes dryer to toss in a towel to warm for after the baby's bath. Molly's peals of laughter pleased Tobie straight to her toes.

"Ready," Clay announced, turning off the water. "Let's get her undressed."

Tobie perched on the edge of the bathtub, the baby clutched in her lap. Clay knelt on the floor in front of them and unsnapped the buttons of Molly's jumper.

The image of this man, tall and strong, tenderly undressing the small, delicate child, ripped a hole of yearning through Tobie's very soul. Oh, how she wanted this! A sweet infant, a husband who assisted with the daily details of child care. Would such happiness ever be within her grasp?

Molly wriggled as Clay tickled her lightly, pulled off the soiled jumper and dropped it into the corner. During the process of disrobing the baby, his muscled forearms rested on Tobie's knees. She sucked in her breath through clenched teeth, shocked at the erotic sensation produced by his touch. Only the thin silken barrier of her evening dress separated their bare skin. The cool porcelain bathtub beneath her bottom provided a sharp contrast to the riotous fire building deep within her lower abdomen.

The bathroom seemed to grow smaller, closing in on them until a panicky sensation descended upon Tobie. What on earth was she doing here, tempting fate? She knew she could never become involved with a man like Clay Barton. He was too much like her whimsical, ne'er-do-well father. Despite his tenderness with the baby, his low-key sense of humor and his exceptionally fine body, Tobie could not, would not allow herself to succumb to his charms.

A good daddy he might make, but what kind of provider would he be? He was a thirty-year-old man who sat in his apartment all day tinkering with some pie-in-the-sky invention. How could she commit to someone like that? With Clay, what you saw was what you got. He had no ambitions beyond perfecting a glorified trash compactor! Was she asking too much? Seeking someone who possessed Edward's hard-working, dependable qualities, yet hungering for a man who loved children as much as Clay Barton did.

Schooling her features to display a nonchalance she did not feel, Tobie shifted her weight, trying uselessly to distance herself from Clay. He seemed oblivious to her uneasiness. Leaning in closer, he removed Molly's diaper, his warm breath tickling the hairs on Tobie's arm.

"Come here," he cooed, holding his arms wide, and for one breathless second Tobie thought Clay was speaking to her.

Molly cooed in return and blew drool bubbles. She kicked her arms and legs with vivid delight, her little eyes never faltering from Clay's face.

A surreal sensation enveloped Tobie. She felt as if she were outside herself, watching the scene unfold. She saw Clay's fingers, lean and powerful, lifting the baby from her lap. She admired the big kiss he dropped on Molly's cheek. She breathed in the sweet baby scent clinging to her clothes and mixing with the smells of mashed potatoes and strained green beans.

"Here we go, sweetpea." Clay knelt beside the bathtub, his shoulders grazing Tobie's leg as he lowered the baby into the water, her body cradled in the crook of one arm.

He doesn't need my help caring for Molly. This man is more capable of fatherhood than many biological parents.

Tobie gazed at Clay. Dusty brown curls trailed down his collar. She suppressed a sudden longing to run her fingers through those touchable locks, to cup the back of his head in her palm. Admiring his profile, Tobie fought the urge to trace her lips over that firm chin, those high cheekbones.

Stop it, Avery. Now! Tobie averted her eyes.

After Clay had settled the baby securely into the tub, he reached over for a yellow rubber duck nesting on the soap dish. The duck whistled when he squeezed it. Molly chortled in reaction.

To her amazement and Molly's elation, Clay began singing the "Rubber Ducky" song from Sesame Street, complete with sound effects. Tobie tried to imagine Edward doing such a spontaneous, lighthearted thing and failed. At the thought of her broken engagement, her spirits lifted. She'd made the right decision.

But just because she was no longer entangled with Edward did not mean she was free to become involved with Clay Barton. For one thing, she knew almost nothing about the man. She'd do well to remember that and keep him at arm's length.

"Could you pass me the baby shampoo?" he asked, looking over his shoulder at Tobie still perched on the edge of the bathtub. "It's on the wall beside you."

Tobie stood and retrieved the baby shampoo. She extended the bottle toward him.

"Get down here and help me," Clay said. "I need all the hands I can get. This kid is slippery when wet."

She hesitated, then bunched her skirt in one hand and knelt beside Clay, her knees sinking onto the damp bath mat.

"I'll lean her back in the crook of my arm," he said. "While you wash the mashed potatoes from her hair."

A startled expression crossed Molly's face when Clay tipped her back in the water. He spoke to her in a soothing voice, and she relaxed, giggling as the water lapped about her ears.

Tobie squeezed a modest dollop of shampoo into her palm and lathered Molly's hair. The baby's eyes grew wide as she looked from Clay to Tobie and back again.

"She's such a little lamb." Tobie sighed wistfully, massaging Molly's scalp.

"Quite a kid," Clay agreed, beaming down at his niece.

"She trusts you completely."

"You think so?" He shot Tobie a quick glance.

Her sweet, violet scent was driving him nuts. How he wanted to rest his head against her shoulder and nuzzle that supple neck. Would she like hot, wet kisses planted there, or would the good doctor prefer a light nip of teeth against her skin. That thought produced an instant tightening below his belt. He had to have this woman. No matter the cost. And young Molly was the girl to help him manipulate Tobie's emotions. Without her, he didn't stand a chance with Tobie Avery and he knew it.

"Are you kidding? Molly's crazy about you."

"Thanks for the compliment," he responded, puffing his chest out with pride. They were crouched over the bathtub, their shoulders touching. Glancing down, he studied Tobie's controlled breathing. Did she feel the same burn of energy as he? Clay swallowed. In the small room, the tumbling clothes dryer generated a lot of heat. Pellets of perspiration materialized on his forehead; he swiped at his upper lip with a shirt sleeve.

The steamy climate left Tobie unaffected. Like a fairytale princess she remained composed, unruffled. She managed to appear regal instead of incongruous, bathing a baby in an evening gown. Straight, jet black hair framed her pale completion and accentuated her delicate features. A gold bracelet glimmered at her slender wrist. Smoky gray shadow shaded her eyelids and her brows had been plucked into perfect arches.

Dr. Tobie Avery was the epitome of cool. Could anything melt Snow White's icy facade?

"Tobie," he whispered.

She raised her head; their eyes met. What Clay saw startled him. The sheer longing in her gaze clutched at his throat and hung on with the intensity of a pit bull. Her chin quivered.

She wanted him!

In that one split second he had read her mind and he knew. Despite her imperturbable disguise, Dr. Tobie Avery was as hot for him as he was for her.

Molly whined, drawing their attention.

"Goodness, Clay, you're getting water in her ears," Tobie scolded. "Hold her higher while I rinse her hair."

Clay obeyed. His pulse thundered through his veins as he held the baby aloft. Molly's whines broke into full-fledged sobs.

"Okay, sweetpea," Tobie said. "We're all done."

Struggling to her feet, she stepped to the clothes dryer and removed the towel Clay had put in to warm. A thoughtful gesture that touched her. How many men would think to heat the towel for after a baby's bath?

He handed Tobie the baby, and she wrapped the tiny girl in the large fluffy towel. Molly's eyelids drooped and she yawned.

"Somebody's getting sleepy," Clay observed, standing up. He dried his hands on his pants leg and reached out to take Molly from Tobie. "You take a shower. I'll put her to bed."

Tobie worried her bottom lip with her teeth. "What'll I wear when I get out?"

Clay longed to say "your birthday suit" but didn't dare. The very idea of Tobie's naked body had him fighting to control his libido. He'd promised her no hanky-panky.

"You can wear one of my T-shirts."

He took the towel-swaddled child and left Tobie standing in the bathroom. Ruefully, she assessed her baby food encrusted evening gown and smiled. She could just imagine what Edward would have to say about her unorthodox appearance.

Reaching around to undo her dress, Tobie discovered the zipper was stuck. Mumbling under her breath, she let out

a yelp of surprise when Clay knocked briefly at the door
and swung it open.

"Sorry. I didn't mean to frighten you. I brought you a
robe and a T-shirt," he explained.

"Umm, could you help me with this zipper?"

They were standing in front of the mirror. Tobie turned
her back to Clay. She studied his reflection as he leaned
over, his concentration focused fully on her stubborn zipper. His angular face took on a studious quality. A lock of
hair flopped down over one eye, and he brushed it away.
Glancing up, he caught her watching him in the mirror and
winked a bad-boy wink. Quickly Tobie jerked her gaze
away and stared at the floor.

His nimble fingers gently worked the zipper down, de-
liberately, slowly, until he'd inched past her bra. Tobie
hitched in a ragged breath. With the clothes dryer off, the
room had lost its warmth. Goose bumps carpeted her skin
and she tried not to shiver.

"Cold?" Clay asked, the heat from his fingers grazing
her upper back as he inched the zipper lower.

"A little," she confessed.

Clay kicked the door shut with his foot. "That better?"

Good gracious, no. She was completely alone with him,
not even the baby for distraction. If she turned around at
this very moment, she would discover herself enveloped in
Clay Barton's embrace. She found the idea very appealing,
and that terrified her. Things were moving too quickly between the two of them. She'd just broken up with her fiancé
tonight, and now she was in another's man's bathroom,
feeling his fingers tickle lightly down her back.

His palm splayed against her bare back, and Tobie
gasped. What on earth was he doing? She heard his ragged
intake of breath.

"What is it?" she whispered.

"I'm holding the top of your dress. It seems the zipper has run off its track.

"Oh."

The coldness invading her body dissipated as fast as it had appeared. In its stead, she felt herself filling with a honeyed heat, her body going limp and pliable as liquid plastic. Did he experience the same deep-down vibrations as she? Heavens. Never in her life had she felt so feminine, so desirable.

"Where's Molly?" Tobie asked in a shaky voice.

"Her playpen. Although with that ingenious kid, I shouldn't leave her alone too long."

"Yes. Perhaps you should go check on her," Tobie agreed. "Thanks for getting the zipper unstuck. I can finish it from here."

"You sure?"

"Oh, yes." He couldn't get out of there fast enough to suit her.

"Okay."

Clay left the bathroom, pulling the door closed behind him. He heard the lock click shut and smiled to himself. Was Tobie Avery as discombobulated by the strange stirrings brewing between them as he?

Did her mouth go dry? Did her pulse race? Did her entire body tremble with the thought of making love to him? If he kept this up, he was going to need an icy shower. How could he possibly keep his hands off her?

But if she did house such feelings for him, why did she constantly erect barriers, both physical and emotional? If only he could persuade her to talk about herself, her history, her broken engagement, then perhaps he could begin to understand that complex woman. Maybe then he could understand the enigma that was Tobie Avery.

Chapter Six

In all his thirty years on the planet, Clay Barton had never been so mesmerized by any woman. Dr. Tobie Avery had taken up residence in his mind, a bewitching squatter who refused to vacate. He did not wish to be so beguiled.

Now wait a minute, Barton, you're the one who coerced her into staying here, he chided. You got yourself into this mess, now get yourself out.

The truth was, he hadn't anticipated this extreme level of attraction for the good doctor. He'd planned on instigating a nice romantic interlude between them, nothing more substantial than that, yet it appeared his maneuverings had backfired in his face. Clay could not stop thinking about her velvet black hair or her pale flawless complexion or those sweet kissable lips. Everything about the woman turned his insides to fire, but it was her innocence that completely undermined his prudence. He wanted her. Whatever the price.

Clay sat on the couch with Molly tucked in the crook of his arm, staring unseeingly at the chattering television set.

He felt invaded, held prisoner by an exotic female who was unaware of her power over him. For years he'd avoided meaningful relationships with the excuse that intimacy was too emotionally costly, too time-consuming, and now it appeared he'd fallen victim to his own tender trap.

Had it been a mere two days since Molly and Tobie Avery had conspired to turn his life topsy-turvy? For the first time in four years, something claimed precedence over his invention.

He heard the shower go on and gulped. His mind detached and wandered from the living room into that damp warm bath with Tobie. Groaning, Clay closed his eyes. He could visualize her, standing naked beneath the nozzle, water pit-patting over her sublime physique, her frilly lace panties kicked into a corner, the smell of her ambrosial scent filling the air like a spring floral bouquet. The image was so vivid, so starkly real, Clay stuck one knuckle in his mouth and bit down hard.

Just then, Molly let out a squeal and promptly kicked him in the stomach.

"Oof." Clay expelled his breath in an agonized whoosh, his desire instantly evaporating. That kid had a mean kick.

Molly jabbered gleefully and grinned at him.

"Dang." He grimaced and rearranged the baby in his lap. "Aren't you a bit young for martial arts?"

She babbled, nodding her head as if she understood every word he uttered.

"Yeah? Well I pity the poor fool who gets fresh with you on a date."

The water in the bathroom went off, and Clay sat up a little straighter. Tobie would be stepping out of the shower now, rubbing herself dry with a terry cloth towel. She'd finger comb her moist hair and slip into his T-shirt, the downy cotton material molding to her superb form.

"Better kick me again," he told Molly. "Your Uncle Clay is in deep trouble."

Tobie wrapped Clay's bathrobe around her and shook her hair free from the towel. Damp tendrils feathered about her face. Folding her evening dress, she tucked the soiled garment under her arm, unlocked the bathroom door and stepped out into the hallway.

She found Clay sitting on the sofa, Molly clutched in his lap. His head was bent over the baby, her bare toes wiggling in the air. Her laughter was high-pitched and delightful. That's when Tobie realized she'd interrupted a game of This Little Piggy.

Something squeezed Tobie's chest. An emotion she couldn't name.

Clay glanced up. He appeared chagrined at having been caught playing a childish game. Tobie thought he looked unbearably sweet.

"Hi," he said, his voice rumbling deep and husky.

"Hi." Tobie grinned like a simpering fool.

His gray eyes meet hers, cloudy as a damp spring day. Tobie felt her face flush.

She set her evening dress in the chair already occupied by her purse. For the hundredth time since she had agreed to spend the night at Clay's apartment, she doubted the wisdom of her decision. Convenient it might be, prudent, no way.

"Have a seat." He inclined his head at the sofa cushion beside him.

Hesitantly Tobie picked her way across the living room, dodging hunks of sheet metal, a box of tools, Molly's stroller and a plastic laundry basket filled with stuffed animals and squeak toys. What a contrast, she thought, Clay's mechanical equipment jumbled with Molly's infantile accoutrements.

Tucking her legs underneath her, Tobie curled up on the sofa beside Clay and Molly.

"Can I hold her?" she asked, extending her arms to take the baby.

"Why, sure." Clay relinquished the child.

Molly fit perfectly in the curve of Tobie's arms. The baby felt soft and snuggly in her little pajamas. Her eyelids drooped and she stuck her thumb in her mouth. "Are you getting sleepy, little one?"

Clay looked at his watch. "Nine o'clock, way past her bedtime. Anne usually puts her down at seven-thirty."

Bringing Molly to her shoulder, Tobie gently patted her on the back. "Your sister will be very proud of the way you cared for her baby." She saw her compliment pleased him.

"I couldn't have done it without you," Clay said. "I really appreciate your help. You've been a godsend."

Tobie couldn't begin to tell him how much he and Molly had helped her. If they had not come into her life she might never have realized how much she wanted children. She might have stayed in her self-delusional haze and married Edward out of neediness. These two had gifted her with freedom. She owed them a lot.

"I think she's asleep already," Clay whispered, leaning over to peer at Molly's face. "Let's go put her down."

"I can't get over how good you are with her. It's amazing." Tobie rubbed soothing circles across Molly's back as she got to her feet and followed Clay into his bedroom where he had the play pen set up as Molly's makeshift bed. "And the baby seems so happy with you."

"Hey." He shrugged. "My sister needed me. What was I suppose to do? Turn her away?"

She looked at Clay's face alight with love for his niece. His mouth softened at the corners as he gazed at the infant. A lump formed in Tobie's throat. Molly was a very lucky little girl. He might be irresponsible, true. He might be a flaky dreamer, but Clay Barton was also the most kind-hearted man she'd ever met.

Tobie laid a hand on his shoulder, and Clay feared he'd break out in a cold sweat from the awesome power of her simple touch. He took Molly from her and carefully placed the baby in the playpen.

"You and your sister must be very close."

"Well," Clay hedged. If he started talking about his family life, he feared he might trip himself in a lie. He wasn't quite ready to reveal his identity to Dr. Tobie. Not just yet. But he had a feeling that this was one woman who would demand complete honesty in a relationship. "We don't get to see each other as much as we'd like."

"That's a shame."

He had to change the subject before she started asking more personal questions. Time to turn the tables.

"You got any brothers or sisters?" he asked.

"No." She shook her head, a sad expression on her face. "I always regretted that."

"There's nothing like family," he agreed.

They both stood there looking at the sleeping child for a moment, then tiptoed out of the room, leaving a lamp on the bedstead burning as a night light.

"You can sleep in my bed," Clay offered. "I'll take the couch."

"Don't be silly. It's your place. I'll be just fine on the sofa."

"I'm something of an insomniac," he warned. "Sometimes I watch television late into the night or work on the recycler. I'd hate to keep you awake."

"You won't bother me, honest. I'd feel terrible turning you out of your own bed."

He wanted to tell her nothing would please him more than to find her in his bed, but Clay decided he'd better not push his luck. Stopping in front of the hall closet, he dug out pillows, blankets and sheets. Making their way back to the living room, they pulled the couch out into a bed and put the linens on together.

"Would you like something to drink?" Clay asked. He was itching to know more about Dr. Tobie. Taking a deep breath, he inhaled her clean soapy scent. "I've got milk, orange juice or cola."

"A glass of orange juice sounds nice." She smiled, and Clay felt as if she'd presented him with a magical gift.

While she settled on the sofa, he traipsed into the kitchen, his heart singing like the Von Trapp family. He poured two glasses of orange juice and came back to the living room to find her wielding the remote control. The channels whizzed by as she rejected one selection after another.

"There's an old Cary Grant movie coming on at ten," she commented, sitting cross-legged on the fold-out couch. "*Arsenic and Old Lace*. It's hysterical. Wanna watch it?"

"Sure. I love old movies. Especially comedies."

"Me, too." She beamed.

Tobie looked like a high school girl in his oversize T-shirt, her face devoid of makeup. Dressed like a teenager at a slumber party, no one would take her for a licensed physician.

He handed her the glass of orange juice and started to sit on the floor. She patted the bed beside her. "You can sit here."

"You sure?" His pulse galloped at the thought of getting so close to her.

In answer, she scooted over. The metal springs creaked as he crawled in next to her, feelings as if the gates of heaven had just swung open to admit him. Was Tobie Avery finally letting down her austere facade? He liked her this way. Maybe this was the time to push for details of her past, while she was clean from her bath and completely off guard.

"So how come you decided to become a doctor?" Clay asked, kicking off his shoes and stretching out. "As pretty as you are, you could have been a model."

"Looks don't last," she said. "You can't count on them."

"And you can count on medicine?"

"Oh, absolutely. There are always going to be sick people." She paused a moment. "I know I'm suppose to say I adore healing, and that's true, but it's not the reason I became a doctor."

Clay propped his chin in his hand. "What is the reason."

"To support myself."

A shiver of apprehension ran through Clay. Perhaps his first assessment about Tobie Avery was correct. Could the woman be money hungry after all? Maybe she was cannier than he believed. Maybe she already knew who he really was and her attraction to him a mere pretense. After all, his family fortune would put Dr. Edward Bennet to shame. It alarmed Clay to think that might be the case.

"I know. It sounds mercenary, but it's the truth. Fortunately I came to love medicine as well."

"Money's really important to you?" he asked softly, dreading her answer.

"I used to think it was. Now, I know better. What's really important is security."

"Oh?"

"I had a rough childhood. My father was one of these guys who always had some get-rich-quick scheme cooking. And of course he never got rich. In fact, as the years went by, we grew poorer and poorer."

Clay took a sip of his orange juice and waited. In the matter of a few seconds, his opinion of Tobie Avery had altered dramatically. She'd been through a great ordeal, no less traumatic than physical or mental abuse.

"My mother didn't have any skills. Whenever we were up against it, she'd take whatever menial jobs she could find. Waiting tables, cleaning houses, working in sweat shops." Tobie had a faraway look in her eyes as she related her tale. "Daddy moved around a lot. Just when I'd start to make friends, he'd uproot us again."

"I can't imagine it," Clay commented, thinking about his plush Tudor home in West Over Hills.

"Once, we had to live in a tent. Daddy never would take a real job. He was convinced one day he'd strike it rich."

Sorrow angled through Clay at the thought of what she had suffered. While he'd been raised on gourmet food, private schools and the best life had to offer, poor little Tobie had been living in abject poverty. Good thing her father was already dead; Clay had a bone to pick with that man. "I guess he never found his pot of gold."

Tobie shook her head. "When I was fifteen he had a heart attack and died. Mama and I were left nothing but funeral bills. We had to go on welfare. From that day on I swore I would never sink that low again. No matter what I had to do."

As she spoke, she huddled like a frightened child at the painful memories, her shoulders hunched forward, her head held low. Clay murmured his sympathies as she continued. "I studied hard all through high school and won a scholarship to college. I chose medical school because I knew doctors made a nice living. I also swore no child of mine would ever suffer as I had."

Clay shuddered at the image of his defiant little Tobie taking on the world. He could not begin to imagine how harsh her childhood must have been.

"That's what attracted you to your fiancé, isn't it? His ability to provide you with a stable environment."

Tobie sighed. "I never acknowledged that to myself before yesterday. But yes, I suppose so. Edward was everything my father was not. Successful, responsible, a man of his word."

"So why did you break up with him?" Clay asked.

"He didn't want children." Tobie's voice caught. "After I saw you with Molly, how tender and caring you were, I knew I couldn't marry a man that didn't want kids."

"Did you love Edward?" Clay whispered, holding his breath.

"Love? Ha." Tobie let out a harsh laugh. "Like Tina Turner says, 'What's love got to do with it?'"

"Why, everything." He stared at her in surprise. "It's suppose to be the reason people get married."

"My parents were madly in love, and look where it got them. My mother so adored my father she'd put up with anything he dished out. Whenever he'd come home with a new scheme she'd bat her eyes at him like he hung the moon and actually encourage him!"

"When you love someone, you put your faith in them," Clay said.

"Even when they fail you repeatedly?" Tobie snorted. "I don't think so."

"Then you still believe money is the key to a good relationship?"

"No. I never wanted riches. Not really. I only wanted a father who went to work every morning and brought food home at night. I simply wanted to live in a modest house, make lots of friends and never be lonely or hungry or homeless." A tear slid down her cheek.

"Here, here," he said, reaching out to put an arm around her shoulder. It felt so good to touch her, so right. "Everything's okay now. You're a doctor, you've got a place to live, food to eat."

"But I don't have a family of my own." She sighed. "It's just my mom and me."

"Give it time," he whispered, flicking her tear away with the pad of his thumb. "You'll achieve your goals eventually."

"I didn't mean to unload on you," she apologized. "Who am I to complain?" She waved her hand. "I'm sure things weren't easy for you, either."

"That's completely all right. You can cry on my shoulder anytime." He held her against his chest, marveling at the softness of her skin, the warmth of her body. How had he survived thirty years without this, without her.

"You're teaching me a lot about life, Clay."

"Me? Like what?"

"That stability and dependability can spring from other sources besides money. The way you are with Molly has shown me that. You're an honorable person, Clay Barton." Her eyes glimmered as she spoke.

Guilt zinged through Clay. He didn't know how to respond. He'd painted himself as a poor man to play on her sympathies, to enlist her help with Molly. He had wanted to see if Tobie Avery would fall for him and not his money. He had not expected to unearth her tragic past. How in the world was he going to tell her the truth? That he was wealthy beyond her wildest dreams. That he was not an honorable man. That he had lied to her.

The dilemma chewed at him. If he confessed his transgression he'd risk alienating her, yet under the circumstances how could he continue the falsehood he'd so glibly perpetrated?

"Tell me about your childhood, Clay. How come you're not married with a passel of kids?"

She drew her knees up under her chin, wiggled her perfectly manicured toes. Clay saw her nipple buds strain at the cotton material of his T-shirt. He swallowed. How he

longed to caress those supple breasts. Inwardly he groaned.
Either he could spill his guts and come clean, certainly
forsaking the chance to explore her lissome contours further, or he could hedge her questions for the moment, buying time until he could think things through and formulate
the best approach.

"I'm obsessed with perfecting the recycler," he said
truthfully. Or at least he had been until he'd met a certain
raven-haired physician. "It's not fair for me to get married
and have a family and then neglect them for my inventions."

"That's very wise," she said. "You shouldn't have children until you're ready to sacrifice your dreams in order to
make theirs come true."

"You'll make a great mother someday, Tobie."

"You really think so?" She beamed at his compliment.

"Absolutely."

"You never did answer me about your childhood." She
rested her head on his shoulder and gazed up at him. She
looked so innocent, so trusting. Lying just inches from his
were her lovely red lips. Her violet scent invaded his nostrils, claimed his senses. "Is Anne your only sibling? What
are your parents like? Where did you grow up?"

They were back to deep water again. He had to divert
her attention. "Look," he said, "the Cary Grant movie is
starting." Reaching for the remote control, he turned up the
volume.

"Oh, forget the movie, we're having a great discussion."
She splayed a hand across his chest.

Clay gulped. "Be right back. Got to go to the bathroom."

He slid off the fold-out couch, feeling suddenly bereft at
severing their connection. But if he stayed, he'd have to
kiss her. And kissing would lead to other things. Already
a fire burned deep within the most masculine part of him.

A flame Tobie had stoked and Clay feared no other woman could ever extinguish. He wanted her so desperately his body ached with throbbing need.

And for the first time since he'd met her, Tobie had seemed truly relaxed. She'd felt comfortable enough with him to reveal her most damning secrets, and he'd been unable to reciprocate.

He shut the bathroom door behind him and sank against the wall. Good thing he had escaped before things had escalated out of control. God, how he'd wanted to make love to her.

If she knew the truth about him, would she want him? And if she did want him, would it be for his money?

Stepping to the sink, Clay turned on the faucet and splashed cold water in his face. Conflicted, Clay ran a hand through his damp hair, toweled his face dry and sighed. How had things gotten in such a mess?

Tobie watched him disappear down the hallway. Anxiously she bit her bottom lip. Why had he evaded her questions about *his* childhood? What was he hiding? She'd been completely honest with him, why couldn't he open up to her? Surely his childhood could not have been any worse than her own.

On the other hand, perhaps his reluctance was for the best. Things had been moving far too quickly between them. Good heavens, she'd lain in his arms! He'd wiped tears from her face. If that wasn't a prelude to intimacy she didn't know what was. Even after a year with Edward they'd never shared anything as close and confidential as what had just transpired between Clay and her.

At age twenty-nine Tobie was still inexperienced in the ways of lovemaking. For so much of her life she'd focused on achieving her goals that she'd never had time for men or dating. Then Edward had never seemed interested in consummating their relationship before marriage. A fact that had left her relieved.

But here, tonight, in the comforting circle of Clay's arms, she'd been prepared to explore a physical relationship with him. That realization stunned her. Was she crazy? She barely knew the man. Yet the attraction between them was that powerful. She'd been prepared to ignore her common sense and heed the urgings of her body. Tobie had never felt so wanton or so foolish.

Ashamed of herself, Tobie decided the best course of action was to pretend to be asleep when Clay came back from the bathroom. She'd promised him she'd stay the weekend and help out with Molly, but she'd make up an excuse and back out of the arrangement. Given her feelings for the man, how could she stay?

Stretching out on the sofa bed, Tobie buried her head in the pillow. It smelled of him—robust, honest, faintly metallic. She heard the bathroom door click shut. Slowing her breathing, she lowered her lashes to narrow slits and peered down the hall at him.

Clay opened the door to his bedroom and stood at the threshold. Tobie realized he was checking on Molly. The loving action tore at her heart. When she told him he'd taught her a lot over the course of the past few days, she'd meant it. Since her association with Clay she'd come to comprehend what real dependability and stability were about. All the money in the world could not buy the tenderness, the unconditional love he felt for his niece.

Most of her life Tobie had equated stability with financial security. That was just plain wrong. Look at Edward. He was rich, powerful and yet at his inner core he was poor, penniless in the things that mattered.

Growing up, she'd always blamed her father's lack of money-making abilities for the pain she'd suffered, when in reality it was his reluctance to relinquish his crazy dreams for the welfare of his wife and child that hurt the most. If her father had ever once put their concerns first, Tobie knew she could have dealt with the poverty.

The floorboards creaked under Clay's weight as he made his way back to the living room. She let her eyelids shutter completely.

"Tobie?" he whispered. "You asleep?"

She did not answer. It was better this way, to feign sleep and let them both off the proverbial hook.

His hand grazed her leg, and for a panicky moment Tobie thought he was caressing her. But the assumption was shattered when she heard the television click off, and she realized he'd simply been reaching for the remote control. Disappointment surged through her veins. What was the matter with her? Did she want him to touch her or not?

Rustling noises piqued her curiosity, followed by the thwap, thwap of sheet metal. What was he doing? She didn't dare risk opening her eyes for fear he'd catch her. Suppressing a yawn, Tobie lay still until at last she drifted off to sleep.

Some time later a screeching sound jerked her awake. Confused, she sat upright. Where was she? Blinking, Tobie rubbed her eyes and looked around. Oh yes, Clay Barton's apartment. Glancing at her wristwatch, she saw it was 2:45 a.m. The sofa bed groaned as she swung her legs over the side, her gaze scanning the room.

The sound reoccurred, drawing her attention to the corner where the Barton Home Recycler sat.

"Clay?"

His head popped up from behind the contraption, a pleased grin on his handsome face. Just the sight of him had Tobie catching her breath.

"I'm sorry, did I wake you?"

"What's going on?" She got to her feet and slipped into his terry cloth robe before crossing the room.

He was hunkered down behind the recycler, the back removed from his invention. Machine oil soiled his right cheek, his hair stuck out at odd angles as if he'd been repeatedly running his hand through it. His body quivered with excitement.

"I think it's finished," he whispered, as if speaking louder would ruin that reality. "Four years of my life I've poured into this project, and I've finally perfected her." Sentimentally he ran a hand over the top of the machine. "I can't believe it."

"That's amazing." Her father hadn't even come close to realizing any of his dreams. Perhaps Clay was a visionary after all and not just a hopeless dreamer.

Pure pride shone from his eyes. "When I started this proposition I knew I wanted to create something that would help the environment. I was appalled by the wanton destruction of the rain forests, the ever-widening ozone hole. I was determined to do my part."

"That's an honorable goal."

"Ready to test drive her?" he asked, still touching his creation with loving fingers.

"You want to share this moment with me? Shouldn't your parents be here? Or your sister?"

"Tobie, I can't think of anyone I'd rather try out the recycler with than you."

His words flattered her. The biggest accomplishment of his life and he wanted to bestow the honor upon her. What a kind gesture. She was touched.

"I did a dry run," he explained. "That was the noise that woke you. Now I'm ready for some actual trash." Tobie giggled. He met her eyes and grinned. "I'm nervous as all get-out."

"I have confidence in you." And to her amazement, To-

bie knew that she did. Was this how her mother had felt
when her father proposed his wild schemes? That thought
gave her something to consider.

"Thanks." The lock of hair flopping across his forehead
gave him the appearance of an adorable little boy. "Come
on, let's go dig in the wastepaper basket."

He held out his palm, and she slipped her hand into his.
She could feel the depth of his excitement. He tugged her
into the kitchen behind him and swung open the cabinet
door under the sink. Retrieving the paper bag that served
as his trash sack, he hauled her back to the living room.

"Okay," he said breathlessly. "Start feeding the trash
in." He handed her the sack and lifted the lid to the recycler. "One thing at a time. Don't want to overload her
at first."

Tobie pulled a plastic orange juice bottle from the sack
and dropped it down the shute.

"Here goes." He flipped the switch, then pointed a finger at her, indicating she was to keep feeding in refuge.
The machine gurgled like a garbage disposal.

Next Tobie inserted an aluminum can.

Clay pushed a flashing green button. The machine emit-
ted a different sound.

"Try glass," he instructed.

Clenching her teeth, Tobie dug in the sack until she
found a cola bottle. "Are you sure?"

He nodded. "Might as well put her through the
wringer."

"You mean the recyler, don't you?" They looked at
each other and grinned. Tobie popped the bottle down the
shute.

Clay hit the yellow button beside the green one. Once
again the noise changed, this time sounding something like
a meat grinder.

"Now what?" Tobie asked.

"Pray that it works."

They both held their breath, waiting. The machine dinged like a clothes dryer completing its cycle, and the lights flashed off. Clay knelt on the floor and opened one of the two doors in front.

He extracted a pellet of plastic roughly the same size and shape as chicken feed. His face glowed. "There's one." Passing the pellet to Tobie, he opened the second door.

The plastic was still warm in her hand. She stared at it, stupefied.

"Here's the aluminum." The can had been transformed into a thin, flat sheet of foil.

"Clay, this is unbelievable!" Her own enthusiasm built, almost matching the flushed, electrified expression on his face.

"Now for the finale." He breathed.

He lifted a small cylinder from the center of the machine and, standing up, held the tube out for her to survey. The substance inside looked like sparkling sand.

"Glass?" Tobie marveled, arching her eyebrows in disbelief.

Clay nodded. "It was the hardest to perfect."

"This is extraordinary! Oh Clay, I'm so proud of you!" Tobie threw her arms around his neck and kissed him squarely on the lips.

Although she'd taken him by surprise, Clay responded quickly, fumbling to set down the cylinder then grabbing both of her wrists and pulling her to his chest.

Tobie gasped, shocked by the intensity of his reaction. His mouth came down on hers like an avalanche—monumental, majestic, overwhelming.

She'd never been kissed like this before.

As if a lighter had been flicked, their kiss simulated the dynamic combination of flame and oxygen. Higher, hotter, more savagely their passion churned as they drank thirstily from each other's lips.

His firm masculine hands burrowed beneath the hem of her T-shirt, creeping upward to cup her tender breasts in his callused palms. His tongue plunged the hungry cavern of her mouth.

She allowed him entry. Courted his touch.

The very center of her womanhood exploded, crying out to be sated. She yearned to fuse with him, longed for their bodies to become as one. She had never given herself to a man. Had never known what it was like to truly be a woman. His molten embrace gave her a glimpse into that magical world, and she wanted more!

Until this moment, in the throes of his untamed ardor, she had not realized what he meant to her. This was the man she'd waited an entire lifetime for. Her partner, her better half, her soul mate. Clay Barton was all these things and beyond.

But he was also the man who did not trust her enough to disclose his innermost thoughts and secrets. When she had opened herself to him and revealed her deepest fears, he had refused to reciprocate, instead had held back a part of himself. How could she enter into the ultimate physical closeness with him when he could not willingly give her the emotional alliance she needed?

Molly's shrill cry shattered their embrace, saving Tobie from the rash action that might have ruined her life. Blindly she pushed Clay away. Stumbling from his grasp, she ran down the hallway to soothe the sobbing baby. Pushing through the bedroom door, Tobie took Molly from the play-pen and pressed the child to her, relieved yet saddened that things had ended this way.

Chapter Seven

The sound of Clay's footsteps vibrating against the parquet floor corresponded with each thud of her heart. A steady throbbing that pulsed through her ears, louder and harder with every advancing step.

He was coming for her.

Cowering in the middle of the room, Tobie clutched Molly to her chest, her eyes trained on the door. How could she face Clay? What would she say to him?

One last step. The bedroom door creaked loudly. Her breath hung in her throat.

She looked up.

His body filled the door, blotting out the hallway light. In the shadows he appeared alien, his expression somber and dark. Tobie trembled. Who was this man? She had kissed him with heartfelt fervency, yet she knew almost nothing about him.

His eyes met hers, and to Tobie's surprise she saw pain reflected in those turbulent depths.

A long moment stretched into painful silence. Tobie dropped her gaze but kept a firm hand on Molly.

"Are you afraid of me?" he asked at last.

Was she afraid of Clay? He was a paradox, at once honest and secretive. And just as her father had, he'd tossed aside society's expectations of manhood to pursue a dream. But Clay was different from her itinerant parent. He had proven himself with the marvelous invention sitting on the living room floor. Tonight he had shown her in a stark manifestation that he was a man of his word.

Yet beneath his persona smoldered a rebel. She spotted it in the cocky way he slouched against the doorjamb, the way his hungry eyes raked over her body. Everything about him set her on fire: his voice, his touch, his warm breath on her neck.

What would it feel like to make love to this man? Her mind conjured a track she did not want to follow, an image of their bodies entwined as they generously gave of themselves to each other. Mouth against mouth, skin against skin, man against woman.

"Tobie?"

She did not answer.

In two strides Clay covered the space between them. Reaching out a hand, he cupped her chin and guided her face up to meet his.

"Are you afraid of me?" he repeated.

No. She was not afraid of Clay. Rather, Tobie was terrified of the feeling rioting in her mind and body like unknown entities.

"No," she whispered.

"Then why did you run from me?"

She shrugged helplessly, unable to voice her thoughts.

"I would never make you do anything you didn't want to do."

"I know."

"Things got a little heady in there, a bit out of control."

"Yes."

Molly cooed and curled a hand around Tobie's ear. The baby's damp fingers tickled.

"Just wanted to let you know you're completely safe with me if you want to go back to sleep."

But did she want to be safe from his heated touch? That was the ultimate question. She could easily become addicted to the sound of his laughter and his agreeable nature. He was a balm on a painful burn, soothing, healing. Just being in the same room with him made her feel more positive about herself.

"Thanks." Tobie forced a smile.

He took her hand and guided her over to the bed. "Here. Snuggle up in my bed." He pulled back the bedspread.

Still holding Molly, Tobie slid between the sheets, arranging the baby beside her. Clay tucked the blanket around them. Snapping off the night light, he settled down into a chair beside the bed.

"Aren't you going to sleep?" Tobie whispered. Clay's wristwatch glowed a luminescent green.

He shook his head. "But you get some rest. You've got to go to work tomorrow."

Tobie burrowed into the covers, breathed deeply of Clay's scent trapped among the cotton fibers. Molly curled into the curve of Tobie's body, made fretful noises, then finally fell asleep.

Lying in the darkness, she listened to the reliable sounds of Clay's breathing and her heart filled with longing. It felt so good, so right to be here. She'd finally found the place where she belonged, but did she have the courage to reach out and grab it? Or would fear paralyze her with indecision?

Clay dozed a little, jerking awake before dawn. Exhilarated, he stared at Tobie's sleeping form snuggled under the covers, little Molly nestled next to her. During the course of one night, two dramatic earth-shattering things had occurred.

After years of research, hard work and fierce determination, he'd created a valuable machine. His long-held dreams had culminated in an invention that served to better mankind. Pride knotted his chest, the triumphant sensation of a job well done.

And Tobie had shared the moment with him.

Tobie. Thinking of her, he smiled into the darkness. When they'd kissed, something incredible happened. Something that had stolen his breath, addled his mind, fogged his senses. He'd ached with the overwhelming need to consummate their passion. Had burned with a longing so strong he tasted it in the back of his throat. He wanted her as he'd never wanted another. The craving he experienced stretched far beyond the physical plane. He wanted all of her. Not just her gorgeous body but her heart, soul and undying commitment as well.

When he began his campaign to lure Dr. Tobie Avery into his bed, he hadn't expected it to end this way. All he'd wanted was a sweet romantic interlude and nothing more. But the reality of knowing her had changed things drastically. He could not blithely take of her generosity, her sincerity, her purity. Tobie was an exceptional woman and she deserved to be treated that way.

He had to win her. And that meant telling her the truth about himself. Revealing that he was Clay Barton, heir to a vast oil and gas fortune, would alter her perception of him. How to go about admitting he'd purposely deceived her was his dilemma. Wincing, he shifted in the chair, stretching his arms and rotating his neck to ward away kinks. Perhaps it might be best to wait until he patented the recycler, then he could come to her, a self-made man, garnering her respect and hoping against hope that he could capture her love in return.

* * *

"Hi, honey."

"Hi, Mom."

Her mother's voice drifted over the phone lines. Tobie smiled at the sound. Two years ago, her mother's employer, a retail clothing boutique, had sold out to a conglomeration. Stella Avery had accepted a promotion as district sales manager and had moved to company headquarters in South Carolina. Although they didn't get to see each other as often as Tobie would like, they still had a close rapport and talked on the phone at least two or three times a week. But since meeting Clay Barton, Tobie hadn't had a chance to call her mother and let her know what had been going on in her life over the past several days.

"What's happening in your world?"

"Funny you should ask," Tobie said. She was sitting in her office, the phone receiver tucked under her chin. "I've got a lot to tell you."

Clay and Molly had given her a ride to her condo early that morning where she'd changed clothes and packed a suitcase. They'd waited in the car while she made morning rounds at the hospital, then they dropped her off at the office. At the prospect of spending the whole weekend with Clay and Molly looking at cars, her stomach churned.

Remember, she reminded herself, you're only doing this because you need transportation.

"Sweetie I'm calling to see if you and Edward might be free next week. I'm coming to Fort Worth and I thought we could all have dinner."

Tobie bit down on her lip. Was it only yesterday that she'd called things off with Edward? It seemed ages ago.

"I broke up with Edward," Tobie blurted.

"Oh. Well, how do you feel about that?"

"Happy."

To Tobie's surprise, her mother agreed. "I never thought Edward was the right man for you."

"How come you never said anything?"

"And be accused of interfering?" Her mother chuckled. "You're a grown woman, Tobie Lynne, I can't tell you how to live your life."

"Why didn't you like him?"

"I never said I didn't like Edward, but I was afraid you were marrying him to ensure financial security. I watched you try to convince yourself you were in love with him."

"How did you know?" Tobie leaned back in her chair.

"Silly girl. I've been in love. I know what the real thing feels like. I know the way a woman looks at a man when she's truly, madly, deeply in love. You, my dear, never looked at Edward that way."

"I don't know if I believe in love," Tobie mumbled, but her heart swelled with thoughts of Clay. How could she love a man she scarcely knew? She'd come to the conclusion that the strange attraction she held for the him was good, old-fashioned lust, and nothing else.

"Fiddlesticks. That's a load of fairy dust and you know it. You're just afraid to let yourself love."

Tobie twisted the telephone cord around one finger. Maybe her mother was right. Maybe she was afraid of falling in love, of losing control, of ending up a prisoner to her emotions. Had she subconsciously chosen Edward for that very reason? The thought was disconcerting. His cool, unruffled countenance had promised a calm, secure life.

"You know how I felt about your father," her mother said softly. "He was my soul mate. My other half. As much a part of me as an arm or leg."

"Yes," Tobie replied. "And Daddy left you destitute, and his death almost destroyed you. I never want to hurt like that."

"Darling," her mother chided, "you're missing the

point. Without some pain, you can never know true joy. Everything I went through with your father was worth it. I loved him. Nothing else mattered. Not surviving on a shoestring, nor moving from town to town, nor all the emotional highs and lows of living with a creative man. What you don't seem to realize is that I had complete faith in him.''

Did she have faith in Clay? After last night, after he'd proven himself with the recycler, yes. But before that? Tobie nibbled her lip.

''Dad let you down.''

''I truly believe in the very depths of my heart, if your father had lived, he eventually would have achieved his dreams.''

''Mother, you're living in a fantasyland.''

''Perhaps.'' She sounded hurt, and a twinge of guilt shot through Tobie. ''But marrying your father was the best thing that ever happened to me, and without him I would never have given birth to you.''

Tobie said nothing. What was there to say? She untwisted the phone cord from her finger and got to her feet. A bubble of loneliness built inside her. A sad feeling so achingly bittersweet, she tasted it. Would she ever know undying love? Did she really want to?

''Don't worry, honey,'' her mother continued. ''I have a premonition you're going to meet the right man soon.''

She almost told her mother about Clay, but prudence stayed her tongue. Tobie wasn't prepared to talk about the budding relationship, if indeed the situation between Clay Barton and her was a relationship at all. She'd been there when he'd perfected his invention. Momentous joy had precipitated that passionate burst between them. It certainly wasn't something on which one built a future.

In her imagination she saw Clay and his rakish smile. He winked at her, Molly cocked on his hip. Tobie shook her head. No. Best to keep quiet about him. If her mother thought Edward was all wrong for her, Clay Barton would most certainly spell disaster. He was capricious, irresponsible and unstable as nitroglycerin. Any sane woman getting involved with him was just asking for heartbreak.

But he's so good with children, the voice in the back of her mind echoed.

"Well dear, I think you made the right decision about your engagement to Edward. How about I meet you for supper Monday night? When I was cleaning out the attic, I found an old strongbox that belonged to your father and I'd like to talk to you about it."

"Oh?"

"Yes. There were some interesting papers inside. I've got to consult a lawyer, but I think I might have some good news."

"Mother stop being so mysterious. What's up?"

"I'd rather not say right now. But I'll see you Monday night."

"All right, Mother." Her mother's evasiveness piqued her curiosity.

"It's a date."

Tobie hung up and stared at the phone. What was her mother hinting at? Lilly's knock on the door tugged Tobie from her reverie.

The girl stuck her head in the door. "Your eight-fifteen is here," she announced, and popped back out.

The morning passed quickly, with over a dozen sick patients to see. Spring pollen wreaked havoc on allergy sufferers. While Tobie wrote out prescriptions for antihistamine and antibiotics, her thoughts never strayed far from Clay Barton and his startling invention. Last night, when they'd realized the recycler truly worked and worked well, the flush of excitement had been so intense neither of them could resist tumbling into each other's arms.

The heady potion of success had stirred their passion. That and nothing more.

Liar. Who was she kidding? Deluding herself about the depth of her feelings was not the answer. She had to find a constructive way to deal with this.

Breaking for lunch, Tobie tried to empty Clay from her mind. She had to stop spinning fantasies about the man. The sum knowledge she possessed concerning Clay was his propensity toward babies and his love of contraptions.

Unfolding their relationship demanded sharing. Before things went further, she had to know the real Clay Barton. She wanted to hear about his hopes and dreams. What childhood circumstances had molded the independent man? Where did he get his aptitude for inventing? And what was responsible for his nonconformist attitude? Somehow Tobie felt that if she understood Clay she might have an inkling into understanding her father.

"You've got a visitor," Lilly announced over the intercom as Tobie washed her hands after the last patient.

Tobie's heart leapt; her stomach fluttered. Clay. He'd said he and Molly might come by to take her to lunch.

Toweling her hands, she cleared her throat and pushed the intercom button. "Send him in," she said, then scurried to her desk. Bending over, she took her purse from the bottom drawer. She ran a comb through her hair and applied lipstick. Straightening, she smiled.

"No need for that, you look beautiful just as you are."

"Edward?" Her smile froze "What are *you* doing here?"

An enormous bouquet of at least three dozen yellow roses preceded her ex-fiancé into the room. As always, Edward Bennet was impeccably dressed in a thousand-dollar suit, his hair perfectly styled. "I've come to win back your affections," he announced, striding across the room to confront her.

Tobie stood beside the desk, her hands clenched. He stopped in front of her desk and extended the flowers. Openmouthed, she accepted the armful.

Edward's hands curled around her shoulders. "I must have been crazy to let you walk out on me last night."

"I don't think this is the time or place to discuss our engagement."

"Please, darling, I know I've neglected you. I'm so sorry. Let me plead my case. Sit down."

He pulled her chair out and waved a hand for her to sit. Still holding the flowers, she plunked down on the wheeled desk chair.

"This isn't going to work—"

"Shh." He laid a finger over his lips. "Hear me out."

Tobie sighed. "All right."

"After you departed, I entertained some deep contemplation about the nature of our relationship."

"You did?"

"Yes. Particularly when my guests arrived and everyone missed your captivating presence."

Ah-ha, here was the truth. Edward missed her because her absence had been noticed by his society pals. He despised embarrassment of any kind, went out of his way to avoid social gaffs. Hosting a party without her had placed him in the realm of improper etiquette. Funny how she could suddenly see his motives so clearly now.

"Listen, Edward, I appreciate—"

"No, no." He interrupted her a second time, holding up a soft hand that contrasted sharply with Clay's rugged, callused palm. It shocked Tobie to realize that at one point she'd seriously considered sharing her life with this man. "Allow me to continue."

Closing her mouth, she laid the flowers on her desk, leaned back in the chair and waited.

"Tobie you are an exquisite gem, and I must have you

as my bride. If that means I have to start a second family, then so be it."

"Are you offering to have children with me, Edward?"

"That is correct." He clasped his hands behind his back and waited, his eyes never leaving her face.

"I'm sorry, Edward, but no."

A startled expression crossed his face as if he hadn't considered the possibility of her refusal. "I beg your pardon?"

"I said no."

For once the sophisticated physician was at a loss for words. "Er…well, maybe you could reconsider."

"I don't love you, Edward. I thought I did, but I now know I did not. Love and security are not the same things."

He looked as if she'd dealt him a solid blow straight to the solar plexus. "Then my original contention must be the real reason you left me."

"What's that?"

"You've found someone else."

"You're darn tootin' she has!"

Tobie and Edward both swiveled their heads to stare at Clay Barton standing in the doorway, Molly clinging to his neck, one thumb stuck in her mouth. The sight of them had Tobie's heart singing.

Edward's eyes narrowed as he turned to face Clay. The two men sized up each other like wary roosters circling for a fight.

Thrusting out his chest, Edward glared down the end of his patrician nose at Clay.

The difference between the men was acute. Where Edward was formal in his flawless suit and expensive Italian loafers, Clay was beyond casual in faded blue jeans torn at the knees, battered sneakers and a skintight T-shirt that read: Lead, Follow, Or Get Out Of The Way. Edward held himself with the prim dignity of royalty, while Clay affected a bad-boy slouch.

The dissimilarity deepened. Edward's haircut was exact, not a hair out of place, whereas Clay's unruly locks proudly announced the carefree windblown look. Even their speech delineated their opposition. Edward uttered stiff, well-thought-out words. Clay said whatever was on his mind.

With the two of them paraded out in front of her, there was no comparison. Clay Barton was the one who made her pulse pound, her breath shallow. His was the image etched into her mind.

Edward represented material wealth, security, stability. Clay personified simplicity, spontaneity, freedom. All her life Tobie had convinced herself she wanted what Edward could offer, while in her heart she desperately needed the things only Clay could provide.

How could she have been so wrong for so long?

Clay rounded the desk with the calculated nonchalance of a predator stalking his quarry, placing himself between Edward and Tobie. Even with the baby latched onto his side, Clay looked deadly.

"Tobie's with me," he announced, and she had no urge to contradict him.

"Do I know you?" Edward asked, pointing a finger.

"I don't think so."

Edward shook his head. "I've seen you somewhere before."

"You must be mistaken," Clay said firmly.

Shifting his gaze from Clay to Tobie, Edward cleared his throat. "Is it true? Are you with *him* now?"

"Yes," she said, unprepared for her own answer. It was the truth. The experience they'd shared had altered her in irrevocable ways. "It's over between us, Edward. I'm sorry if I've hurt you."

"Are you sure, Tobie?"

"You heard the lady," Clay growled.

True to his nature, Edward refused to rise to the fight. Lifting his chin, he stopped long enough to scoop the roses off her desk. Turning, he left with aplomb.

"So that's Dr. Edward Bennet," Clay said, once Edward had disappeared from view.

"Yes, but I would have preferred to handle things my own way."

"What in the heck did you see in him?" Clay pulled a face.

His gloating, cock-of-the-walk manner irritated her. She was finished with Edward, yes, but she still hadn't made up her mind about Clay. Then it occurred to her, Clay was jealous.

"Edward's very structured and dependable, unlike some people I could name." She leveled him a cool glance.

"Oh-ho, is that a jab at me?"

"Take it as you will."

"Face facts, Tobie, you were attracted to Dr. Bennet's moolah, plain and simple."

"That's not true," she denied. How could one man infuriate her yet excite her at the same time?

"It doesn't matter. Ancient history. Let's go to lunch," he said, extending a hand.

She hesitated. "I don't know if I want to go anywhere with you." She turned her shoulder to him in a haughty gesture.

He perched on the edge of her desk, Molly resting against his right side. Leaning over, he hooked one finger under the stethoscope dangling around her neck. He tugged on the plastic tubing, pulling her ever so slowly toward him as if she were a coy catfish and he a patient fisherman.

The action was erotic, sensual. Helplessly Tobie let him entice her forward. She could jerk back and the stethoscope would pop free from her neck, but she didn't. Caught up, a kite in a high wind, she followed his movements, allowing herself to be sucked in by his mesmerizing charms.

"I could kiss you right now, Dr. Tobie Avery," he growled, low and throaty.

Part of Tobie thrilled to Clay's assertion of masculine power, but conversely, her more prudent side cautioned discretion. The implications of the last few minutes floated through her mind. She needed time alone, to think and re-evaluate her options.

She was about to send him on his high handed way, when Molly grinned and held out her arms. Tobie melted. She could refuse the baby nothing.

Allowing Clay to tug her to her feet, she took Molly from him. He slid his arm around her shoulder. The sensation felt good. Too good. She squirmed away.

He looked wounded by her withdrawal but said nothing Tobie led the way out of her office and down the corridor. "See you after lunch," she told Lilly.

The receptionist lifted her hand in a bewildered wave. With Clay trailing behind her, Tobie pushed through the clinic's front door and out into the bright spring sunshine.

"You're miffed at me," Clay stated once they were out of Lilly's earshot.

"You do think highly of yourself, don't you?"

"Hey." He grinned and shrugged. "If I don't, who will?"

"You're assuming a lot about me, Clay Barton, and I don't like it."

"I thought after last night we sort of had an understanding."

"Where did you get that idea?" She balked beside his jalopy, cupping one hand around Molly's chubby leg. "Just because a girl kisses a guy doesn't mean he owns her."

Clay came around and opened the car door for her. He

stood oh so close and smelled like charged ions during an electrical storm—sharp, musky, stimulating.

"We experienced a hell of a lot more than a kiss, Tobie, and you know it. That's why you're running scared." Their eyes locked. He lowered his head.

Tobie suppressed a shudder of delicious anticipation. Was he going to kiss her again?

"You don't own me, Clay." She tossed her head.

"I feel as possessive toward you as I do for Molly," he said, his voice husky. When he reached out a hand to brush a lock of hair from her cheek, Tobie jumped as if burned. "I feel as if we've known each other our entire lives."

"Well, we haven't. You keep yourself hidden from me, and you know it. I told you about my childhood, my hopes, my dreams, my mistakes, but you never reciprocated. You want me to fall for you, but you don't dare give yourself to me. It's a two-way street, Barton."

"I'm not hiding anything." He chuckled but the laugh was weak. He looked downright suspect, confirming her suspicions that there was something in his life he did not want her to know about. "Come on, Tobie," he coaxed. "Don't be mad."

"Then talk to me."

"I will." With a swoop of his hand he indicated the open car door. "You ready?"

Installing Molly into her car seat, Tobie noticed a wicker picnic basket on the floorboard. "What's this?" she asked, easing into the passenger side and buckling her seat belt.

"It's such a beautiful spring day I thought you might like to eat in the park." He gave her a brilliant smile, and despite her better judgment, Tobie forgave him everything. "I thought we'd have a spring celebration."

She studied his profile as they drove the short distance to a small park. The man was such a paradox. One minute strong and forceful, his chin firm and uncompromising, as when he'd stared down Edward Bennett. This was the tenacious side of him that kept him plugging on with his inventions long after lesser men would have surrendered. But in the next moment his jaw would soften and he'd appear gentle, conciliatory as he had last night after she'd fled from his embrace...the tender way he was with Molly.

"Here we are," Clay announced, stopping the car at Winston Park. They unloaded the baby and the picnic supplies, then trailed over the moist, green lawn to a shady spot beneath a budding oak tree.

The cerulean sky, the dancing daffodils, the butterflies flitting from blossom to blossom, conspired to produce a pristine picture of springtime in Texas.

While Tobie held Molly, Clay spread a blanket on the cool ground. When he finished, she sank to her knees. Molly babbled, squirming to be set free. Tobie settled her onto the blanket. The baby squealed with glee and wiggled her bare toes in the warm breeze.

Clay lifted the basket lid and extracted sandwiches wrapped in wax paper. "Ham and cheese, or chicken salad?" he asked.

"Chicken salad. Did you make the sandwiches yourself?"

"Yep."

Of course he'd made them. On his tight budget, Clay probably couldn't afford deli takeout.

"Champagne?" he asked, removing a bottle of bubbly from the basket.

"Just a tiny bit. I do have to go back to work."

He peeled off the foil wrapping and popped the cork. Champagne fizzed down his hand. The sound, the dry smell of champagne, brought memories to Tobie's mind. How many nights had she lain in bed dreaming of the days when she'd sip champagne and eat caviar on the French Riviera? She smiled at her childhood whimsy. Eating homemade chicken salad sandwiches in the park with Clay and Molly was a million times better than her fanciful ideas of fortune.

Tobie caught a peek at the champagne label. Expensive stuff. How could he afford it?

"I've had this in the fridge for years," he said as if reading her mind. Wiping his hand on a paper napkin, he poured two plastic glasses half-full and extended one to her. "Just for a celebration like this. The recycler, springtime, Molly and you."

Ducking her head to hide her reaction to his sweet words, Tobie took a sip of the heady beverage.

"A toast?" he held up his glass.

Scooting closer, she rested the rim of her glass against his.

"To Tobie Avery. The woman who was there when I needed her most."

His sentiment stirred tears within her. She swallowed hard, fought back a fierce blush. "I can't take any credit," she protested.

"You've been a godsend with Molly," he said firmly. "Here's to many more inventions shared." He clinked his glass against hers again.

What was he saying? The implication of his statement caused an odd sensation to hug her chest. Goodness, she wanted that, too!

"Yep, we hope Dr. Tobie stays around for a long time, ain't that right sweet Molly Malone?"

The baby, happily chewing on a teething biscuit, grinned.

They sipped champagne and nibbled on chicken salad sandwiches. Tobie's thoughts whirled, crazy as the champagne bubbles. She was so attracted to this man, and yet her rational mind ordered extreme caution. She felt trapped in a maelstrom of conflicting emotions.

"This is the best celebration I ever had," Clay said.

"Oh?" Tobie teased. "You're used to elaborate bashes, eh?"

"Yes." He shook his head. "You should have seen the wingding my parents threw when I patented the No Drip Faucet. They invited the most prominent..." His voice trailed off.

"What?" Tobie prompted. "I want to hear. If chicken salad sandwiches with me and Molly is the best celebration you ever had, I want to know about others."

"My folks invited all their friends, and we barbecued in the backyard," Clay finished up the story, realizing he'd almost spilled the beans about his parents. He couldn't tell her that a United States senator had been among the guests as well as movie stars and a world-famous lawyer, or that the catered affair had cost six thousand dollars. Despite the hoopla and exclusive guest list, he'd meant every word when he told her this private celebration with Molly and her meant more to him than the most showy extravagance his parents could conjure.

Sooner or later he knew he was going to have to tell Tobie the truth about his identity, but not now. Not until after he'd patented the recycler, when he could prove to her he was a respected man in his own right, not merely his father's son. Besides, if he told her now, she might be too angry to spend the weekend with him and Molly. Clay couldn't risk that.

The dry, sweet taste of champagne clung to his tongue as he tucked their empty glasses and the discarded wrappers into the picnic basket. Stretching out, he laced his fingers together and cradled the back of his head in his palms.

Mockingbirds trilled their repertoire of songs. Redbirds and blue jays swished through tree branches. A squirrel raced across the lawn, his tail bouncing as he ran. Clay caught Tobie watching him from the corner of her eye.

"Come here," he said, holding out an arm to her.

She hesitated only a moment before allowing him to tuck her into the warm curve of his body. They lay nestled together, watching Molly crawl about on the blanket.

At that moment, with Tobie's violet-scented hair teasing his nostrils and the sound of his niece's laughter floating on the breeze, Clay felt completely content. In two days' time he'd be traveling to Houston to see a patent attorney with his invention in tow.

He was whisper close to achieving his dreams. A recycler in every home. A wife in his own. Wife? Had his thoughts really progressed that far where he and Tobie were concerned?

Rising up on one elbow, he looked down at her. She blushed like a bride, shy, hopeful. He dipped his head and claimed her lips, remembering the intensity of the night before, when it had been all he could do to keep from taking her to bed. But she hadn't been ready, and now he was glad. Tobie was a special lady, and he wanted their ultimate joining to be something special.

The kiss was light, feathery, undemanding. She looked up at him, her blue eyes wide.

One drink from her lips was enough. For now. He settled back down on the blanket and drew her closer. "Look at the clouds," he whispered. "I see a cowboy riding a horse."

"This is a dreamer's game," she said.

"What do you mean?"

"My dad used to play it with me. He saw lions and castles and dragons. I just saw clouds."

"Aw, come on, squint your eyes and try real hard." He pointed at the sky. "Doesn't that look like a horse? See the proud head? The galloping hooves."

"No. Sorry, Clay, I'm just not the whimsical type."

"That's okay," he whispered. "Somebody has to have their feet on the ground."

With her head resting in the curve of his arm, Clay admitted what he felt for her was the most overwhelming emotion he'd ever experienced.

What did she feel for him?

The question caught in his throat. She wanted him, he knew that much. But beyond physical attraction, he couldn't say. But she was here with him and not Edward Bennet. Chuckling to himself, Clay tried to imagine the stuffy plastic surgeon lying on a blanket, baby drool on his shirt. No way, no how. He most definitely had the edge in that respect.

Still, it worried him that Edward had shown up at Tobie's office attempting to woo her back. Would he try again? Would Tobie have succumbed to Edward's charms if he and Molly hadn't arrived when they did?

"This has been a really nice lunch, Clay, but I've got to get back to work," she said, breaking the spell the spring afternoon had woven. Sitting up, she brushed wrinkles from her skirt.

"You are coming back to my apartment tonight, aren't you?" He got to his feet and gathered up the picnic supplies.

She hesitated, and his heart tripped.

"I don't know if that would be such a good idea," she murmured.

"Why not?"

"I'm afraid we'll do something both of us will regret."

"Tobie, please. I need you. Molly needs you."

"No, you don't. You've done a marvelous job taking care of her."

As if in reply, Molly squealed and plucked a handful of grass. She opened her mouth, but Tobie interceded before she could eat it.

"See," Clay said. "With a nine-month-old you can never have too many hands. Please stay." He saw hesitation war with acquiescence on her face, so he pressed. "Remember, I'm taking you to look at cars tomorrow, are you going to make me drive all the way to Candleridge to pick you up?"

"I suppose not." She smiled.

"I'll be the perfect gentleman," he said, holding up two fingers. "Scout's honor."

"Were you really a Boy Scout?"

"No."

"Tell you what, Clay. I'll stay the weekend under one condition."

He had her! She was going to spend the night at his apartment again. "What's that?"

"You tell me exactly what secrets you've been keeping."

Chapter Eight

He'd promised to tell her the truth.

Back at his apartment, Clay changed Molly's diaper and pondered his dilemma. If he told Tobie, he knew she'd be mad and then she'd leave. If he didn't tell her, she wouldn't stay.

Another thought occurred to him. What if he did tell her the truth and she didn't get mad at his deception? What if she was attracted to his wealth? Given her background, growing up in poverty, her engagement to Dr. Bennet, perhaps she'd find his money more alluring than his love. More than once he'd been victimized by a conniving woman angling for the family fortune.

Clay saw no way out. He knew he had to tell her eventually, it was just a matter of timing. Waiting until he patented the recycler would be ideal. That way he could prove to her he could support her despite his parents wealth. That his crazy dreams weren't so crazy. But how to avoid the promise he'd made her in the park?

"Got myself into a regular pickle, didn't I, Miss Molly

Malone?'' He lifted the baby over his head. Her giggle rang out high and light. Reaching out, she touched a finger to his nose.

Love for her swelled in his chest. He cradled his niece tenderly. How wonderful it would be to have a baby of his own, one as sweet and adorable as Molly. He and Tobie would make beautiful babies together.

"Putting the cart before the horse, aren't you, Barton?" he asked himself out loud.

Settling Molly down for her nap, he busied himself with household chores, washing breakfast dishes, running the vacuum, making the bed, all the while his thoughts whirling like helicopter blades. If he could just keep Tobie busy, he might avoid telling her his secret. He knew the problem would arise, however, when Molly was tucked into bed and things got quiet. That's when Tobie would demand emotional intimacy and he would not know how to start.

"Hell," he grumbled. "How did I get myself into this?" He'd never meant to deceive her. He lived his life modestly because it suited him, not because he had some sophisticated seduction scheme up his sleeve. But he feared Tobie would see his deception in that light.

Why did things have to be so complicated? Clay wasn't ashamed to admit he felt bewildered. He liked her, she liked him, things should be fairly simple. But they weren't. Human emotions refused to cooperate in the satisfying way of science and mechanics. He expressed himself through action, not ponderous soul searching.

The hours until five o'clock crawled by. Anxiety mixed with excitement. Anticipation churned his stomach. A time or two, for the sheer fun of it, he ran a few things through the recycler. The process never failed to amaze him, and *he* was the creator. A broad smile played across his lips each time he realized what he had accomplished. It was reality. He, Clay Barton, was an inventor.

By the time Tobie knocked on his front door, he had spaghetti sauce simmering on the stove, a salad in the fridge and a scented bubble bath drawn and waiting. He'd planned to pamper her, hoping to ease his way into the truth.

He opened the door with a flourish, a glass of iced tea in one hand. "Welcome home, Doctor." He grinned.

Tobie looked surprised and tired. Her normally bouncy hairdo drooped, her slender shoulders sagged beneath the weight of her briefcase. Immediately after coming in the door, she kicked her high heels off in the corner. The gesture pleased Clay, she was making herself at home.

"For you." He extended her the tea glass.

"Gee, thanks." She rewarded him with a smile, dumping her briefcase and purse on the couch.

"There's a warm bath waiting for you. Go have a soak while I finish dinner," he invited.

Was it his imagination or did tears glimmer in her eyes. She blinked and swallowed. Had he done something wrong?

"Where's Molly?" she asked as any anxious working mother might.

Quickly Clay scanned the room. "She was here just a minute ago."

In answer, they heard the little girl cry out. Glancing at each other, they dashed into the kitchen where the sound originated.

"Molly!" Clay shouted, ducking his head to peer under the table.

Another loud wail.

Tobie opened the cabinet door to find Molly sitting in the dark among the canned goods. The baby gave them a tearful smile and extended her arms. Clay clasped a hand to his heart as Tobie picked up the baby. Reaching over he ruffled Molly's hair.

"Little girl, you've aged me ten years in four days' time.

I can't keep going through this. I'm putting baby latches on the cabinets tomorrow!" he declared.

"But she'll be leaving in a few days. Why bother with the locks now?" Tobie said, jiggling the baby on her hip. They looked so cute together, he thought. Tobie would make a fine mother someday.

"'Cause I'm not taking any chances with my niece, and besides, I'll probably be baby-sitting in the future. Here, give her to me, and you go take a bath."

Tobie handed him the baby. "It was very thoughtful of you to run me a bath," she said shyly, her eyes lowered.

"You're welcome. Go on." He shooed her in the direction of the bathroom.

The delicious garlicky smell invading the kitchen, the touching sight of Clay with Molly in his arms stirring the spaghetti sauce, the taste of the freshly brewed tea on her tongue tugged at her deepest emotions. Was this what it would be like to be married to Clay? Supper on the table, a clean house, a happy baby. A sexy, caring man.

Intense longing punctured her composure. All these years she'd thought a high-powered, high-profile job represented security, when stability was really depicted by the rock that was Clay Barton. He was kind, hardworking and good with children. So what if he didn't have a regular nine-to-five job. He'd proven himself a fine inventor. Creative types needed a flexible environment and work schedule in order to flourish. Putting Clay in a business suit would be the same as caging a lion—sad and cruel.

Sinking into the bathtub, she closed her eyes and allowed her thoughts free rein. Many men were playing the role of stay-at-home mom these days, and why not? She needed time to adjust. Years of schooling herself to believe she needed an older, well-established husband balked at alternative concepts, but if she wanted a future with Clay, Tobie knew she'd have to change her thinking.

If only he would open up and tell her what secrets lurked in his past. She knew something bothered him, and originally she'd intended to press him for details. But if he wasn't ready to tell her, perhaps it was best if she waited and let him come to her on his own terms. Maybe he was afraid his secret might shock her. That thought bothered her.

Tobie sipped her tea and rubbed a washcloth over her skin. Why delve into his past at all? She knew him for the wonderful man he was today, not for what he might once have been. Did his background account for the hint of wildness she sensed in him? The aspect of Clay that shouted "rebel." Strange, but that dangerous, unknown part of him attracted her as much as his kindness and generosity. The piece of him that promised the exact opposite of stability and security. Was it a similar wildness that had drawn her mother to her father? Sobering.

The weekend passed in a flurry of activity. Early Saturday morning, all three of them ate a quick breakfast, then Clay went to the hardware store for supplies. He spent the next hour or so installing baby latches while Molly and Tobie played in the living room.

After that job was completed, they ate leftover spaghetti for lunch then piled into Clay's jalopy for a trip to the car dealerships. The first location they visited boasted a spring spectacular with clowns and prizes and balloons for the kids. They walked around the lot, a helium-filled balloon tied around Molly's wrist. The baby laughed each time the balloon bounced off the side of Clay's head.

Tobie was uncertain which type of vehicle she wanted. She'd enjoyed driving Edward's sports car, but now she was thinking along other lines. Fast and flashy no longer fit her image. These days she was thinking "family." A nice minivan caught her eye. She tugged Clay over to look at it with her.

"Why do you want a minivan?" Clay asked. "It's too much room for one."

"I'm thinking ahead," Tobie said. "I don't intend to be single for the rest of my life."

"Got anybody in mind?" he asked.

She almost stopped breathing at the hungry look in his eyes. What was he suggesting?

"I mean." He hesitated. "You haven't been reconsidering Edward's offer."

"No," she said, not meeting his gaze. "But I do want to get married and have children someday and not in the distant future."

"Howdy folks!" An enthusiastic salesman greeted them, shattering the tenuous conversation. The man slapped a hand on Clay's shoulder. "You in the market for a new minivan?"

They strolled around the parking lot, looking at vehicles, the salesman chattering constantly beside them.

"Let me guess," the salesman said, waving his hands. "Newlyweds with your first baby."

Tobie started to deny his statement, but Clay prodded her gently in the ribs and shook his head.

"Yes, sir," Clay lied glibly. "How'd you know?"

"The way you two exchange meaningful glances." The salesman bobbed his head. "Anyone can see you're crazy about each other."

Tobie ducked her head. Were her feelings for Clay so blatant a stranger could pick up on it?

"Excuse me, dear," she placed a heavy emphasis on the last word. "Could I speak to you in private a moment?"

"Give us a sec," Clay said to the salesman before taking Tobie's elbow and guiding her behind a purple minivan.

"What's the big idea?" she asked narrowing her gaze

and shifting Molly in her grip. "Telling that guy we're married?"

"Maybe he'll give us a better deal if he thinks we're newlyweds with a baby in the house."

Tobie rolled her eyes. "Listen here, I'm perfectly capable of negotiating my own car deal and I don't have to lie to do it."

"Sir?" The salesman peeked around the corner at them.

"Yes?" Clay glanced at the man.

"I can let this baby go for a thousand dollars off the sticker price." The man patted the purple minivan. "Believe me, I know what a struggle it is getting your feet on the ground after you start a family. Me, I got three kids of my own."

Clay shot Tobie an I-told-you-so look.

"Do you have something a little less purple?" Tobie asked.

"You betcha. Blue, white, silver, black. Follow me." The salesman started off across the lot. Clay took off after him but Tobie grabbed his jacket and hauled him backward.

"Hey, smarty pants, how am I supposed to buy a car with you?" Tobie asked. "This is my car and my money, remember?"

"Got that covered," Clay assured her. "We'll just tell him you want the car in your name so you can establish credit."

"I already have credit, thank you very much."

"Tobie, the guy's already offered to come down a thousand bucks and we haven't even started haggling. That's a pretty good deal."

Tobie paused. She had to admit he was right. What would it hurt to pretend to by Mrs. Clay Barton for a few hours?

"Ready to make a deal, wife?"

Wife. The word sounded so good on his lips. A tingle

shifted down Tobie's spine when he linked his arm with hers and guided her inside the showroom. When they emerged an hour later, Tobie was the proud owner of a brand new powder blue minivan. The salesman told her she could take delivery of it on Monday.

"Okay. So you want to go for a test drive, wife?"

Wife.

They took Molly to the zoo, and the rest of the afternoon passed in a blur of laughter and good conversation. Clay touched her often, taking her hand, resting his arm across her shoulder, patting her knee. She felt breathless and giddy with each display of affection. She'd worn blue jeans, a white cotton blouse and a peach-colored blazer. Several times she caught him appraising her with an admiring glance. No man had ever made her feel so feminine, so wanted.

He talked of the recycler, and Tobie listened intently to the joy in his voice. This weekend was a special one for him, as well. This week had ended in the culmination of his lifetime dreams, and she'd had the good fortune to share it with him.

They rode the train around Forest Park. Clay sat with Molly in his lap, his arm around Tobie. Leaning into the curve of his shoulder, Tobie breathed deeply of the late-afternoon air, scented heavily with aroma of roses, tulips, honeysuckle and daffodils. Right here, right now, her life felt completely perfect. All too soon Monday would come and she'd have to go back to her silent condo and frozen TV dinners. Abject loneliness seeped through her marrow at the thought.

As if sensing her changing mood, Clay leaned over and lightly kissed her temple. Instantly her body responded, jolting her with pinpricks of happiness.

Clay made her happy, she realized. He was a poor, strug-gling inventor who might never make enough money to support a family, but Tobie didn't care. She was a physician, she could support her own family. All that mattered was that Clay and his niece had brought inexplicable joy to her life.

Finally, about seven o'clock, they trudged back to Clay's apartment. Tobie took Molly to the bedroom for a diaper change, while Clay busied himself preparing her bottle.

Molly was greedily sucking down her formula, tucked in Tobie's arm like a precious china doll when the phone rang. As Clay talked, Tobie cooed to the baby girl and smoothed her hair with a finger. She couldn't wait for that glorious future day when she would become a mother.

"That was Anne," Clay said, coming into the living room with two glasses of cola. He set one down in front of Tobie, then seated himself next to her. "Holt's mom is doing much better. She and Holt will be home tomorrow."

Tomorrow? Tobie's stomach sank to her feet. That meant she no longer had an excuse to stay at Clay's place. It would be time for her to return to that quiet, empty condo she called home. In fact, with Molly gone, she'd have no reason at all to ever see Clay again.

"Tobie?"

She looked at him, swallowing back the tears that blocked her throat. Molly had fallen asleep, the weight of her head resting in the curve of Tobie's arm.

"Are you all right?" In an instant he was down on his knees in front of her. He took her hand in his. "What's wrong?"

"Nothing." Her voice came out high-pitched and nervous. How could she tell him her heart was breaking at the thought of never seeing them again? "I'm glad your sister's mother-in-law is doing better, and I know Anne and her husband will be so happy to see Molly."

"You're going to miss her, too, aren't you?" He rubbed her fingers.

"Yeah. Silly, I know."

"No, it's not," he said fiercely. "I'm going to miss her, too. I've gotten quite used to this little scamp rearranging my life." Lightly he traced a finger along Molly's jawline. "Let me have her, I'll put her to bed."

Clay eased Molly out of her lap and took the baby to the bedroom. Tobie sat fighting the emotions rioting within her. Who would have thought Molly could have affected her so deeply?

"Wanna feed the recycler?" Clay asked upon his return. Rubbing his hands together in anticipation, he shot her an endearing look.

"Sure." She smiled, knowing just how much the strange contraption in the corner meant to him.

Lovingly, he caressed the machine. "I still can't believe it really works."

Tobie got off the couch and came to stand beside him. "What do you plan to do with the money you make from the recycler?" she asked, watching him flip the switch and feed a paper bag through the slot. The machine gurgled and clanked.

"Oh, I don't know," Clay mused. "I thought I might buy a motorcycle and take a trip cross country. I haven't had a vacation in four years."

"What?" She frowned.

He rocked back on his heels. "I take it you don't approve."

"It's not my place to tell you how to lead your life."

"What would *you* have me do with my money?"

"Well, I'd certainly recommend something less frivolous." She looked down her nose at him.

Her haughty countenance irritated him. Just who did she think she was? Little Miss Aster?

"You should consider investing in mutual funds," she continued. "Something reliable."

"And boring."

"There's nothing boring about making money."

"Probably not to you."

"What's that suppose to mean?" She sank her hands on her hips and glared.

"It means that constantly worrying about financial matters kills the life out of creativity. That's why I wanted to travel the country. To pump the old creative well."

"I find that attitude irresponsible."

"Why don't you just come out and say it. I'm the one you find irresponsible. Admit it."

"If the shoe fits." She tossed her head. The fiery expression in her eyes lit a corresponding fire in his abdomen. Dr. Tobie Avery might be cool and collected on the surface, but underneath her professional facade blazed the heart of a passionate woman.

"Ha! I knew it. You tried not to let my lack of money matter, but it does, doesn't it?"

"I never said that."

"You thought it."

"I merely stated I believed it irresponsible of you to fritter away any windfall you might receive from your invention like some James Dean wannabe. For heaven's sake, Clay, you're thirty years old. You should be thinking about the future."

"Why? I don't have a family to support."

"You might someday."

"I'm not like your father, neglecting my kids so I can achieve my dreams. If and when I have children, you can rest assured they'll be taken care of. Not forced to sleep in tents."

Tobie drew back as struck. Tears sprang to her eyes. Miserably, Clay wished he could retrieve those ugly words but it was too late.

"Ah, Tobie, I'm sorry." He reached for her, but she spun away. "I didn't mean it."

"I opened my heart to you, shared the bitterness of my childhood and you use it like a sword against me. I should have known I couldn't trust you when you keep secrets. I was a fool to think this relationship had possibilities."

Had she, too, been thinking about continuing the alliance they'd forged over the past few days? Had he ruined his chances with her forever?

She trotted across the room and began retrieving her things.

"Please," he said, "you don't have to go tonight."

"I think it's best."

"It's late. You're tired."

She stood there, trembling with anger. Her purse over one shoulder, her briefcase clutched in her hand.

"I'm sorry," he apologized. "Truly." To tell the truth, he wasn't quite sure why she was mad. Because he'd planned to spend his money frivolously or because he'd insulted her father? Both probably. Open mouth, insert foot. He kept forgetting how important money was to her. It was a symbol of everything she'd never had as a child. Whereas he had the opposite approach to riches. He'd been raised with the trappings of wealth and found it stifling. He longed for the freedom the simple life offered. How could he tell her that without revealing to her who he really was?

"Let's not end our weekend like this," he said.

"Better to leave now than drag things out," she replied.

All the old doubts she'd had about Clay came creeping back. She'd told herself it didn't matter that he had an untraditional job, that the success of the recycler had proven him to be more than an irresponsible dreamer. And because the feelings she had for him were so intense, so frightfully close to love, she'd convinced herself it was enough that he would make a great husband and father.

But when he'd spouted his plans for riding a motorcycle across the country, her prejudices had reared their ugly heads. Motorcycles equalled undisciplined teenagers or third-rate hoodlums. If he was going to make a career as an inventor, he should begin immediately on a new project, not dilute his momentum by taking a prolonged vacation. Did he care nothing for structure or stability? Did he, like her father, enjoy the uncertainty of a hand-to-mouth existence? Or was she setting her standards too high? Did she expect too much? With Edward she'd had all the things she'd ever wanted. Except love and the possibility of children. Two things she could not live without.

Blowing out her breath, Tobie ran a hand through her sleek hair. Would she ever be free from the restrictions of her childhood? Could she ever learn how to be spontaneous and natural like Clay?

He looked so forlorn, like a big puppy dog who'd lost its best friend. She suddenly felt very ashamed of herself. Clay Barton had a way of ruffling the cool visage she'd spent a life time perfecting. It was as if she were made of glass and he could see through all her pretensions and defenses. And try as she might she could not deny the fact that in his arms, she felt such a sense of rightness. Like she had always belonged there.

"Please," he repeated. "Stay here. It'll be your last chance to see Molly."

He certainly knew her weakness. With a sigh, Tobie dropped her briefcase and tossed her purse in the corner.

"You win," she said helplessly.

Tobie woke to the smell of bacon and coffee. Rolling over, she stretched and smiled.

It was nice, she realized, to be pampered and spoiled by him. She'd never experienced this before. With Edward, she'd been the one doing the pampering.

Molly babbled from her playpen in the corner. The baby pulled up on the railing and grinned at Tobie, wriggling with happiness to find her there.

"Good morning, sunshine." Tobie threw back the covers and padded over to lift Molly up. "Goodness, somebody's got wet pants."

After they'd changed—Molly into a dry diaper and undershirt and Tobie into a pink print sundress—she toted the baby into the kitchen. Spying Clay in his pajama bottoms, flipping bacon with a fork, Tobie felt suddenly shy.

Molly squirmed to be let down. Bending over, Tobie settled the child to the floor. Faster than a road runner, the baby crawled across the linoleum, her little legs working like windmills. She encountered a wall, turned and crawled back, her peals of laughter filling the apartment.

"Good morning," Clay said, his voice rumbling deep and sexy. His hair was in disarray. He gave her a lopsided grin. "How did you sleep?"

Tobie couldn't help smiling back. "Like a baby."

"Hopefully *you* had dry pants."

Tobie's mouth dropped open. Grabbing a dish towel off the kitchen table she twisted it in her hands.

"Now, now." Clay dropped his fork and raised his palms. "You wouldn't pop an unarmed man, would you?"

"You asked for it." Grinning, Tobie bounced on the balls of her feet, shifting her weight like an edgy boxer. "Come on, Barton, make my day."

Ducking, he dodged the flick of her towel. "Jeez, Avery, you're awfully frisky this morning. Have a good dream last night?"

"Okay, that's it, you've had it." Wielding the towel, she chased him around the kitchen until they were both laughing and breathless.

"Truce! Truce!"

"No mercy," she cried triumphantly and cornered him.

She twisted her towel, took aim and popped him right on the bottom.

"You stinker," he exclaimed, grabbing her wrist and pulling her to his chest.

Tobie dropped the towel; her heart accelerated. They stood nose to nose, chin to chin, mouth to mouth.

She heard his sharp intake of breath.

"What you do to me, woman, should be a crime," he whispered hoarsely, his hand tightening around her wrist.

"Oh, yeah?" She thrust her chin forward, literally daring him to kiss her.

"Yeah." His lips came down on hers, possessive, hungry, demanding.

Her free hand trailed to his nape. She spurred him on by tangling her fingers in his hair and tugging lightly.

"I knew it," he murmured, pulling back.

"What?" she asked, leaning up to capture his bottom lip between her teeth.

"That beneath that professional cool lurks the heart of a wildcat." He wrapped his arms around her waist. Lowering his head, he kissed her again.

"Hmm," Tobie commented, enjoying his minty taste.

"Good thing you didn't kiss me like this last night," he panted, burying his face in her hair. "I couldn't have been held accountable for my actions."

"Are you trying to say you're a bit of a wildcat yourself?" she growled low in her throat.

"Ah, Tobie, you're too damned sexy." He placed a palm on either side of her face and planted his mouth on hers once more.

She felt the kiss in her toes. Tilting back her head, she allowed him deeper access. Untamed desire stirred her womb. Her entire body vibrated with needy urgency. She wanted Clay Barton to make love to her!

Molly's high-pitched keen tore them apart.

"What is it? Where is she?" Clay exclaimed.

Tobie bent to pick the baby off the floor, her head still reeling from the force of what had just transpired between them. Her lips burned; her blood pulsed; her loins ached.

"What is it?" Clay demanded again. He seemed as disoriented as she felt.

Tears rolling down her cheeks, Molly held out her little hand to Tobie. The index finger was red and turning purple at the nail.

"She smashed it in the cabinet door," Tobie said, ducking her head to kiss Molly's sore finger.

Clay plowed a frustrated hand through his hair. "That's why I installed those baby latches, so she wouldn't get in the cabinets and hurt herself."

"It's the way the latches are designed." She shook her head. "They only keep the door partway closed. A baby can still get her hand inside."

"I ought to invent better ones," Clay fumed. "Poor Molly."

"She'll be okay," Tobie said, smoothing down the infant's hair. "One of many lessons to be learned in the journey of life."

"Why, Dr. Avery, I didn't know you were a philosopher," he teased. Then his eyes widened as he stared at the stove. "Good grief, the bacon's burning."

Stepping over one of Molly's wooden blocks on the floor, he snatched at the iron skillet with his bare hand.

"Clay," Tobie called out to stop him, but it was too late.

Yelping he dropped the pan back down on the stove top. Acrid smoke filled the air. Molly sneezed.

Tobie turned on the faucet. "Get cold water on your hand. Now."

Clay stumbled over Molly's blocks, let loose with a howl of pain, then hobbled to the sink to douse his burned hand.

Coughing against the smoke, Tobie turned off the burner and clicked on the stove's fan.

"Open the door," Clay suggested, wincing.

With Molly perched on her hip, she scurried to open the front door, then returned to the kitchen. Using a dish towel to fan smoke out of the kitchen, Tobie glanced in Clay's direction.

"Are you all right?" She raised her voice to be heard over the fan's rattling hum.

"I'm fine."

"What a mess."

"The three stooges make breakfast."

"You calling me a stooge?"

Clay grinned.

"Anybody home?" A strange female voice drew Tobie's attention from Clay. She looked up to see a stylishly dressed young woman standing in the doorway between the kitchen and the living room. The woman wore gold jewelry and designer clothing. Very classy. Behind her stood a tall man with a bemused expression on his face. Who were these people? Tobie wondered.

"Holt! Anne! You're back." Clay sounded nervous.

Instantly embarrassed, Tobie combed her fingers through her hair, aware of how things must look—the kitchen stinking of charred bacon, Clay bent over the sink, his hand under the cold water faucet, tear streaks staining Molly's checks.

"Looks like you've had your hands full, baby brother." Anne picked her way across the kitchen floor to give Clay a big hug.

He turned off the water and dried his hand on the towel Tobie pitched his way. "We didn't expect you back until late afternoon."

"We caught an early flight," Anne said, taking Molly

from Tobie. "I couldn't wait to get home and see my precious angel." She smothered her baby with kisses.

The tall man followed his wife into the kitchen. He smiled at Tobie and extended his hand. "I'm Holt Johnson and this is my wife, Anne. I understand you've been helping Clay take care of our little Molly."

"Yes," she replied, not knowing what else to say. She was surprised by the aura of affluence about these people. From their expensive clothes to their cultured mannerisms, Anne and Holt Johnson radiated the self-confidence of old money. Quite a contrast to Clay and his humble abode. Tobie couldn't help wondering why Anne didn't help her brother financially. Clay was probably too proud to take handouts, she surmised.

"This is Dr. Tobie Avery," Clay said, slinging an arm across her shoulder.

"Thank you so much, Dr. Avery, for intervening when Clay got in over his head." Anne smiled and touched Tobie's shoulder. "He was supposed to hire a..."

"Do you think it'll scar?" Clay interrupted, shoving his hand between the women for their assessment.

Tobie shot Clay a suspicious glance. Something wasn't right here. Was it her imagination or did he seem excessively flustered. She studied his palm. Nothing worse than a first-degree burn. The skin hadn't even blistered.

"You'll live," she said.

"Come on, Anne, Holt, let me help you gather up Molly's things." Clay spoke quickly. He bent to snatch Molly's blocks and blanket from the floor before herding everyone toward the living room.

"We really do appreciate all you've done," Holt said, taking his turn at hugging his daughter. "It was a relief knowing Molly was in good hands while we were at the hospital with my mother."

"Yes," Anne agreed. "I wish you hadn't gotten stuck, Clay. If only Mom and Dad weren't—"

"Out of town," he finished for her. "Did I tell you guys the recycler works?"

While Clay chattered to his impressed relatives about his invention, Tobie studied him. He spoke hurriedly, his body language tense as a soldier on alert. She frowned. Clay was definitely hiding something. He'd interrupted his sister twice, and he seemed determined to usher them out of the apartment as soon as possible. Not for the first time she wondered what secret he was keeping.

Holt and Clay loaded up Molly's belongings while Anne repeatedly hugged and kissed her daughter. Clay kept casting glances at Tobie and his sister as if reluctant to leave them alone in the same room together. His actions had Tobie longing to corner Anne and ask her a million questions about Clay and their childhood, but each time she tried, Clay would come flying back into the room, alert and breathless, his gaze darting from Tobie to Anne and back again.

Tobie shot Clay a warning look. When his family left, she was determined this time to extract the truth from him.

In fifteen minutes the Johnson's luxury car was packed with Molly's accoutrements, and the family was waving goodbye to Clay and Tobie.

The car backed out of the parking lot, and Tobie found herself alone with Clay.

Turning on her heels, she tapped his shoulder. "All right, Barton, spill it. I want to know exactly what it is you don't want me to find out."

Chapter Nine

"**I**'d rather not tell you now," Clay said, perspiration breaking out on his forehead. He'd just spent the past thirty minutes trying to keep Tobie and Anne apart so his sister wouldn't inadvertently spill the beans. "I want the time to be right."

Tobie said nothing, simply stared.

Clay ran a finger around the collar of his T-shirt and tugged at the material. He hated it when she gave him that noncommittal look. What was she thinking behind that cool veneer?

"I—m—mean," he stammered, "I'm not prepared to discuss my problems."

She arched an eyebrow, sank her hands on her hips. Was she never going to say anything?

"I promise I'll tell you everything after I come back from seeing the patent attorney," he said.

Her jaw muscles worked as if she wanted to say something but was controlling herself. Clay hadn't felt so discombobulated since grammar school when he'd been cast in the school play and had forgotten his lines onstage.

"Look," she said at last, "if you're trying to give me the brush-off, just say so. I can take it." She moved past him, heading for the stairs back to his apartment. "I'll just get my things and be on my way. Sorry to have made myself such a burden."

"Whoa, wait a minute, where are you going?" He had to sprint to catch up. Before she reached the landing, he managed to snag her elbow.

"Home." She stood a step above him, glaring down.

"Tobie," he beseeched her. "Give me a break."

Her eyes flashed liquid fire. "Give you a break! What's that suppose to mean? I spent my entire week helping you out with your niece, and you can't even talk to me." She tossed her head. "Worse, you're purposely deceiving me." Her glossy, blue-black hair swung gracefully against her chin. The surge of desire racing through his body left Clay breathless.

"Honey..."

"Don't you dare 'honey' me. We don't know each other well enough for terms of endearment."

"Just because you haven't learned everything about my background doesn't mean we don't know each other."

"Our relationship can never go forward as long as you hide things."

"I'm not hiding things," he denied, but he knew that wasn't the truth. He should tell her the truth. Now. Anything to keep her from walking away. But he was afraid of losing her. Or worse yet, terrified that she'd love the "rich" Clay Barton and forget about the ordinary guy he was at his heart. All his life he'd balked against the opulent image preferred by his family. He'd hated the private schools and exclusive country clubs and overpriced material goods his folks found so important. He saw crystal chandeliers and oriental rugs and priceless paintings as a flagrant waste of money, when there were people starving the world over, and when the environment was being destroyed at an alarming rate.

He wanted nothing more than to invent useful things and gain respect for his own talents, not his parents' money.

"I thought we were working on something," Tobie said. "I guess I was wrong."

"I'm just asking for forty-eight hours."

Tobie tapped her toe against the cement step. "All right," she agreed. "Forty-eight hours. But if by Tuesday evening you don't have an explanation for me, it's over between us. Got that?"

A reprieve! She'd agreed to wait. Now all he had to do was patent the recycler and he'd have something to offer her for the future. Something he'd achieved on his own without the family wealth. Something worthwhile that would benefit mankind.

"You got yourself a deal, Tobie Avery."

On Monday morning Clay guided his aging jalopy down the highway to Dallas. He should have been concentrating on the recycler riding in his trunk; instead Clay couldn't stop thinking about Tobie. From the confident way she crossed those shapely legs at the knees to her sweet floral scent to her pale complexion that easily showed a blush, he could not stop his mind from recalling her image. He didn't understand her at all. One minute she was cool as cucumber salad, the next moment so hot he feared he'd burn his hands when he touched her.

Women. You couldn't figure them. Clay thought in mechanical terms. Cogs and gears made sense to him. Metal and rubber and plastic he could comprehend. But not emotions and most definitely not females.

He knew Tobie was attracted to him. Hell, *attraction* was an understatement. The sparks they generated could set Yellow Stone ablaze, but then at critical moments she'd withdraw into herself, fighting the emotions she felt for him. She could be playful and in the next breath turn deadly serious. And he knew she harbored doubts about his ability to provide for a family.

On some level she perceived him in the same light as her ne'er-do-well father. Obviously Tobie still had some issues to work out with her dead parent. Perhaps Clay should already have told her he was worth millions. That would ease her mind, assuage her doubts, free her to love him. But if he had told her about his finances, he would never know whether she wanted him for himself or his money.

Clay winced at the thought. He'd been caught in that trap before. Once, several years ago, he'd thought himself in love. His heart had been broken by a wily female just interested in the family fortune. He'd found out the hard way when he'd caught her in bed with another man. After his fiancée's betrayal, Clay had sown a few wild oats of his own, never letting anyone get near his heart again.

Until now.

Until Tobie Avery.

Spending these last few days with Tobie and Molly had stirred something deep inside him, had roused a paternal instinct he hadn't been aware he possessed. Clay was amazed at how naturally parenting came to him. In a pinch, he'd come through with flying colors.

Together, he and Tobie had made a tremendous team.

Yes, this past week he'd learned a lot, about both himself and Tobie.

The woman had invaded his mind and set up camp there. With a start, he realized just how much he cared for her. Once the recycler was patented, once he'd proven himself, he could come to her and confess the truth. He could tell her about his money, and hope she'd forgive his deception. Once the recycler was patented, he could tell her how much he loved her. He could offer her a home, a place to call her own, the promise of a family.

His pulse thudded erratically. As soon as he got the patent, he was going to ask Dr. Tobie Avery to become his wife.

Tobie couldn't concentrate. All day at work she'd been distracted. Lilly had noticed and even some of her patients. She couldn't stop thinking about Clay.

Yesterday he'd hustled her out of his apartment as if he'd just learned she had the plague. It was not a pleasant feeling. What had changed? Where had the lighthearted teasing gone? The giddy feeling between them had dissipated with his family's arrival and Molly's subsequent departure. Had Clay only wanted her as a surrogate parent for his niece? Had the kisses they'd shared merely been a pleasant interlude for him? Had she meant nothing more to him than that? And then it hit her, he'd become distant once she started bugging him about the past. Why? Was he hiding something? Did he have a girlfriend lurking in the wings? Or was his past darker than that?

At least she'd had the good sense not to give in to her baser instincts and consummate the relationship. A knot of sadness settled in her stomach. Somehow Clay Barton had managed to find a chink in her armor. Despite her best intentions, he had wormed his way into her heart.

By five o'clock, Tobie was a nervous wreck, trying to second-guess Clay's feelings for her. The intensity of her emotions scared her. How had she let it happen? She'd promised herself she'd never fall for a dreamer like her father, and here she'd gone and done that very thing.

She finished with her last patient at five-fifteen, then went into her office to retrieve her purse and sweater. A knock sounded on the door.

"Come in."

"Hi, honey," her mother greeted her.

"Mom!" Chagrined that she'd forgotten about her mother's impending visit, she moved across the room to give the woman a hug.

"Oh, it feels so good to squeeze you," her mother said.

Tobie stepped back and assessed the older woman. She wore a new designer outfit and a bright smile. "You look fantastic," Tobie exclaimed.

"I have some marvelous news." Her mother's eyes twinkled. "Let me take you out to dinner and I'll explain."

"Sure."

A few minutes later, when they entered the quaint Italian restaurant down the street from the office, Tobie's mother requested secluded seating. "So we can talk," she whispered, clutching a large envelope in her hand.

Once the waiter had seated them and taken their order, Stella Avery placed her hands on the table, palms down. She grinned. "Brace yourself, honey."

"Well, you're smiling, so it must be good news. What gives, Mother?"

Stella opened the envelope and removed some legal documents. "This." She pushed the papers across the red checkered tablecloth to Tobie.

Frowning in the dim lighting, Tobie quickly scanned the papers. "Treasures recovered from the clipper ship, Calypso, sunken off the coast of Brazil in 1778," she read out loud. "It took seventeen years of hard work and dedication on the part of the diving crew and financial backers to resurrect the ancient sailing vessel."

She scanned the rest of the document. It was an itemization of the bounty discovered. Gold medallions, silver tankards, diamonds, rubies, sapphires, emeralds. The catalogue went on, detailing one unbelievable treasure after another. Total value of the recovered haul was estimated at forty-six million dollars.

Tobie looked up at her mother's animated features. "What does this mean?"

"Keep reading," her mother urged, barely able to contain her excitement. She shifted in her seat, drumming her fingernails against the table.

Shrugging, Tobie turned the page and found a list of the investors. She scanned the roster. Suddenly one name leapt from the page to command her attention.

Thomas Delaney Avery. Her father.

Tobie gulped. Her hands trembled. She felt the color drain from her face. "What does this mean?" she whispered.

"Do you remember the year your father invested our last two thousand dollars with a group of divers trying to raise a sunken ship?"

Tobie frowned. "Was that before or after the Indian Reservation fiasco?"

"After. Before the pet rock craze."

Tobie shook her head. "Dad had so many crazy schemes cooking I couldn't keep them apart."

"Well this one turned out to be not so crazy." Her mother tapped the document. "It took Michael Fisher seventeen years to raise that ship, but now that he's done it, we're going to be rich."

Tobie's mouth dropped open. "What?"

"Yes!" The older woman clapped her hands. "He contacted me last week about your father's share of the proceeds. I had to consult a lawyer of course, to make sure everything was all right."

"And?" Tobie leaned forward, unable to believe her father's long-held dream of striking it rich had finally come true, fifteen years after his death.

"Your father's share comes to seven hundred and fifty thousand dollars," her mother whispered. "Can you believe it?"

Stunned, Tobie gripped the table edge with both hands. All those years of struggling and suffering for her father's far-fetched fantasies had finally paid off.

"I always believed in him, always." Stella clasped her hands to her chest and sighed. "I'm just so sorry Tom never got to see this day. I know he felt like a failure, but he was always a success to me." Tears spilled down her mother's cheeks.

"Oh, Mom." Tobie sighed. All those wasted years she held a grudge toward her father, blaming him for her unhappiness. Oh, to erase the past and live it again. How different things might have been if only she had believed in her father as honestly and truly as her mother had.

News of her father's success stirred doubt. Could she give Clay the kind of loyal support her mother had offered her father? Even if he never made a penny from his inventions? Could she stand by him through thick and thin as her mother had? Could she love as intensely, as strongly as her mother? Or had she buried her emotions too deep for too long?

She had financial security. She didn't need Clay to provide for her. His kind of dependability went much further than money. His brand of stability was the type husbands and fathers were cut from. Steady, reliable, good with children, always there in troubled times. Suddenly she couldn't wait for his return. She had so much to apologize for. Would he have her?

Tobie's heart plummeted at the thought of Clay rejecting her. She'd given him an ultimatum and it could very well blow up in her face. The feelings Clay ignited inside her scared Tobie. Their passion burned so strong she'd feared the relationship was doomed to end in charred ashes.

"Honey?" her mother's voice brought her back to the present. "Are you okay? You're pale as a ghost."

"Mom," Tobie said. "I think I've fallen in love and he's just like Daddy."

Her mother's smile widened. "That's wonderful, honey, tell me about your young man."

She twisted the red cloth napkin in her fingers. "Clay's an inventor. A struggling inventor." She emphasized the word *struggling*. "In fact, he's gone to Houston to see a patent attorney about getting a patent for this marvelous machine he's invented."

"Yes?"

"I'm afraid to let myself love him, Mom. I keep remembering what life with Daddy was like. The erratic highs and lows, the financial insecurity, and I just couldn't let myself get close to Clay. But somehow, despite my best intentions, he's captured my heart. I can't stop thinking about him, Mom."

"Do you love him, Tobie Lynne? Because that's all that matters. I know your childhood was not a happy one, and I also know how guilty your father felt for dragging us through the dark fields of his dreams. But he was right." Her mother waved the paper. "He pursued his heart's desire and I followed him. Perhaps we shouldn't have had children. But we both loved you so very much."

"I know," Tobie whispered. "And with me and Clay things are different in one important way. I can support a family. Clay could stay home, watch the kids and work on his inventions while I practice medicine. It's the nineties. Why can't I be the breadwinner?"

"As long as you're both happy with the arrangement," Stella said. "You're never going to have to worry about security again, Tobie. Your father left you that legacy."

Yes, Tobie acknowledged. Things could work between Clay and her. All her life she'd searched for stability, had taken the cautious approach, weighing each risk, calculating her moves. She supposed she'd developed her prudent attitude as a backlash to her father's wandering, carefree ways.

Commitment to Clay, despite his unconventional life-style, would provide her with the security she craved. Around Clay, her anxieties vanished, evaporating in the warmth of his sheltering arms.

"Go to him," her mother counseled, "and tell him exactly how you feel. Life is too short to waste one more minute without love."

Excitement and anxiety fizzed inside Tobie like bubbles in the champagne bottle cooling in a bucket of crushed ice. Clay was due home any minute. She'd driven her new mini-van to his apartment and conned the superintendent into letting her into Clay's place.

Smiling, she surveyed her handiwork.

The table was swathed in a white linen tablecloth. Slender white candles cast romantic shadows. A vase of yellow roses served as the centerpiece. Delicious aromas invaded his small kitchen. Fillet mignon sizzled under the broiler, homemade bread sat cooling on the counter alongside a fresh apple pie. For the hundredth time that evening, Tobie consulted her watch. It was 7:00 p.m. Where was he? He should be home by now.

She'd dressed in a gauzy, white dress and had spent the afternoon at the hairdressers. Her nails were lacquered, her makeup perfectly applied. She was Snow White, waiting for her prince.

If everything went according to plan, she'd surrender her virginity to the man she loved. Her heart thudded with expectation. She'd never purposely seduced a man before. Then again, no man had ever made her feel the way Clay did.

"Oh, Clay." She sighed and sat down at the table.

Her heart raced at the thought of their kisses. If his lovemaking was half as potent as his kiss, she was in a luscious kind of trouble. Shivering in anticipation, Tobie placed a palm to her forehead. If she kept this up, she'd be delirious by the time he got here.

She heard a heavy thud on the steps outside his door. A thrill ran through her. What should she do? Pose provocatively? Meet him at the door? Hide in the bathroom?

More thuds echoed. She frowned, then realized he must be dragging the recycler up the steps.

Relax, she instructed herself. Take a deep breath. But her good advice went unheeded. Her lungs refused to expand. Her muscles coiled like taut bedsprings. The closer the noises grew, the hotter the sensations in her lower abdomen burned.

Waiting, she crossed her legs, fluffed her hair. Finally, after what seemed an eternity, she heard the key turn in the lock. She clenched her fists, swallowed back her anxiety.

Clay wrestled the recycler over the threshold. He stopped, stared. The expression on his face told the story. He was surprised and none-to-happy to see her.

"What are you doing here?" he snapped.

His cold, distant tone cut her to the quick. She had not expected this reaction. She'd come here to apologize for her behavior on the day Anne and Holt had taken Molly home. She'd planned to tell him of her father's belated good fortune. She'd come to say she'd had a change of heart, that she knew she could love him despite the fact he was not a typical nine-to-five sort of guy, that his quirky characteristics made her love him all the more. That she didn't care what secret he harbored. She loved him and they could work through anything.

But instead of being pleased to see her, he seemed angry.

She rose from the table and started toward him. "I...I planned a welcome-home dinner," she stammered, unnerved by the scowl on his face. Where was the jovial, understanding Clay she'd come to love and respect? Who was the brooding man standing just inside the doorway, his hands on his hips, the recycler on the floor in front of him?

"Why?" he asked.

"Something's happened, and I've had a lot of time to think." She paused in the archway between the kitchen and living room.

His gaze raked over her, took in her attire. Shutting the front door behind him, he walked toward her.

Tobie backed up, disconcerted by the savage look in his eyes.

"Why don't you save us both a lot of heartache and leave now," he said roughly.

"Clay, what's wrong? This isn't like you," she exclaimed.

"You don't even know me," he snarled.

Tears welled behind her eyelids. This wasn't going at all like she'd expected. She planned a lovely dinner, a celebration of his patenting the recycler, then a long, slow romantic seduction.

"I…I cooked supper," she said, her bottom lip trembling as she struggled not to cry.

"Turn the oven off. I'm not hungry."

She raised a hand to her mouth. Had she made a mistake? Was the secret he harbored something that made his personality change so severely. Tobie whirled around, her gauzy skirt swirling around her legs. Heading for the oven, she clicked off the broiler. Her chest rose and fell in painful rasps.

His shoes shuffled against the linoleum as he came to lean against the archway. Turning, she watched him fold his arms across his chest and just stare at her. She felt like a germ under a microscope.

"What's wrong?" she whispered. "I'd like to help."

"There's nothing you can do," he said brusquely.

She could comfort him, take him in her arms and soothe whatever tragedy had befallen him. His sorrow was plain to see.

"Tell me," she insisted, wanting to go to him but afraid he'd reject her.

He plowed a hand through his hair. "I don't want to talk about it."

"Is Molly okay?" she asked, suddenly alarmed that something might have happened to the baby.

"She's fine as far as I know."

So the problem wasn't with his niece. Tobie fingered her chin, tucked a strand of hair behind one ear. He should have arrived jubilant over the success of patenting his recycler, instead he was sullen and belligerent. Then it hit her. How many times had she seen these same mood swings in her father? As a child she'd learned to make herself scarce until after his dark disposition had passed following a major failure. From the joyful highs of heightened expectations to the bitter lows of dashed hopes and shattered dreams. Clay must have received bad news at the patent attorney's office, there could be no other explanation.

She went to him then, no longer afraid. Now she understood what generated his sour temper. "Talk to me, Clay. Stop holding back." She reached for him, wrapped her arms around his torso.

His gaze softened but he did not hug her back. "Four years of my life," he said softly, "completely wasted."

"What happened?" she insisted gently.

He let out a harsh laugh. "Yep, Clay Barton, big-time inventor, going to save the world's trash problem with his wondrous recycling machine."

"Stop feeling sorry for yourself." Tobie stamped her foot, using the get-tough approach her mother used on her father when his spirits dived to the floor.

"Easy for you to say, Doctor. When you went to medical

school, you were assured of a steady job, a role in society. Me, I'm just a daydreaming bum."

"That's not true."

"I'm a failure."

She squeezed him tighter. "You are not."

"Yes, I am." He snorted and shook his head, his arms still crossed tightly across his chest despite the fact she held him in a bear hug. "Can you believe it? Someone patented a recycler just like mine not three weeks ago."

"Oh, Clay, I'm so sorry," she said. "But it shows you were on the right track."

"A lot of good that does me. What if I were married with a family to support? Four years spent on an invention and someone beat me to it."

"That's what I came to tell you. It doesn't matter that you're an inventor with an unstable job. I have enough security for both of us," she insisted.

Clay shook his head. "No. You were right all along, I'm just like your father. Irresponsible, daydreaming, self-delusional."

"I was wrong about my father, too," she said. "I saw him through a child's perspective. I only thought about the things he did not provide. Clay, the important thing is, he was doing what he loved."

"To the detriment of you and your mother."

"My father was a visionary ahead of his time. Mother realized that, but I couldn't."

"What are you talking about?" Clay glared down at her. Tobie released her grip on him and stepped back. She took a deep breath.

"I have money now, Clay."

"What?"

"One of the harebrained schemes my father invested in turned out not to be so crazy after all. It took seventeen years to come to fruition, but his investment in salvaging a sunken clipper ship has paid off."

A sardonic smile curled his lip. "Well, Doc, you've made quite an about-face. First you wouldn't get involved with me because I couldn't provide you with a stable future and now you're offering to take care of me. That's a laugh."

Clay's words were true, she had changed because of her association with him and for the better. She no longer judged people for their financial potential. She'd grown beyond that, and she was proud of herself. And her newfound sense of justice had nothing to do with the windfall from her father. His unexpected success had merely illustrated what she'd already learned, that not everything was black-and-white, cut-and-dried. That dreams could come true, and following one's heart's desire was more important than riches. And Clay Barton was her heart's desire.

"I've learned a lot over the past week, getting to know you and Molly," she said softly.

"I wanted your respect, not your pity, Tobie. Until I prove myself for who I am, we cannot have a relationship."

"Baloney! So someone beat you to the patent on the recycler, so what? There will be other inventions, you'll succeed eventually, if you never give up."

"Yeah, posthumously. Sounds great." His sarcastic tone told her he was still hurting.

Strange how they'd switched roles. In the beginning she'd been the one hesitant to get involved with an oddball inventor, while he'd tried his best to charm her. And now that he'd succeeded in garnering her affections, he was the one pulling back, demanding caution.

Well, she'd come here to show him how much he meant to her. She wasn't about to abandon him when he needed her the most. Standing on tiptoes, she angled her head upward and pressed a kiss to his lips.

At first he did not surrender. Angered at his petulance, she took her fingers and pried his hands apart, unfolding them from his chest. She took one of his arms and placed it around her waist, then, lacing her fingers together at the back of his neck, she kissed him again.

"Does that tell you what I think about you?" she murmured.

"You're out of your mind, Tobie Avery. You've no idea what you're getting into."

"Yes, I do. I'm twenty-nine years old, it's time I tasted all life has to offer."

"What are you saying?" he asked hoarsely.

"I came here to make love to you, Clay." She trailed kisses along his neck.

Clay groaned. Things were not yet right between them. He had a lot of disappointment to resolve. He needed to come clean with her, tell her the truth about his family. But how could he now, when he had nothing to offer her beyond his family's name? He'd never succeeded on his own. Indeed, the one thing that had defined him for the past four years had been eradicated in a matter of minutes in the patent attorney's office.

He wanted her. Oh, yes! The thought of their bodies entwined drove him to the brink of tolerance, but this was not the best time to make love to her. Mentally, he knew that, but physically, his body had a mind of its own. Despite his best intentions, he pulled her closer and returned the kiss.

Her presence had surprised him when he'd opened the door. The way she'd acted the last time he'd seen her had him thinking things were over between them. Yet he'd stepped into his apartment to find her waiting for him, dinner in the oven, a romantic table setting. Tobie clothed in the hottest dress he'd ever seen.

Groaning low in his throat, he kneaded her buttocks with

his fingers, enjoying the feel of her soft flesh. She made it so hard to turn her down, but he could not in good conscience take her to his bed. Not until they'd resolved all the things standing between them.

Breathless, he pulled away from her. She clung to him like a shipwreck survivor clinging to a raft.

"I want you, Clay," she murmured, "here, now."

"No," he said harshly, grabbing her wrists and breaking her hold.

She looked up at him, hurt reflected in her big blue eyes. Her bottom lip trembled. "You don't want me?"

"Of course I want you, but not like this."

"What did I do wrong?" She looked down at her sexy dress. Her lips were kiss swollen and tempting. "I thought men liked to be seduced."

He realized with a start she was unsure of her own sexuality. In the beginning of their relationship her kisses had been timid and had gradually grown bolder. Had she no experience? What about her fiancé? Had she never shared the joy of physical pleasures with him? Stunned, Clay acknowledged her inexperience.

"You're a virgin, aren't you?" he said the words, and his heart filled with wonder at the gift she was offering him. A precious prize he could not accept.

She ducked her head. "Yes."

He tipped her chin up to meet his eyes. "Don't be ashamed."

"I'm not ashamed. But I'm ready."

"No, Tobie," he said gently.

Her offer touched him deeply. If he wasn't so in love with her, he'd accept her gift, make love to her "slow, sweet and easy." But under the circumstances he could not take advantage of her. Until he was completely honest, until they had worked out their problems, he could not, in good conscience make love to her.

"Please, Clay, don't turn me away." Tears gathered at her eyelids.

"Tobie, I can't."

"You don't find me attractive?"

"Of course I do. But I've had a bad day, and I've got to rethink the plans for my life. It wouldn't be right to take advantage of you, to use you for my own solace."

The hurt look in her eyes almost made him change his mind. Swallowing hard, he said the one thing he did not want to say.

"I'm sorry, Tobie. Go home."

Chapter Ten

Embarrassment flared through Tobie like nothing she'd ever experienced. Somehow she stumbled out of Clay's apartment and down to her minivan. She didn't even register the trip home. Heartbroken, she staggered into her condo and collapsed across her bed, uncontrollable tears staining her new white dress.

What a fool! She flung herself at Clay like some desperate groupie. She'd thought he was simply feeling discouraged about his invention and that she could ease his suffering with her love. Obviously that wasn't the case. He simply hadn't wanted her, and she'd been too stupid to notice. Finally he'd come out and bluntly told her to leave.

Salty tears blocked her throat. Her nose was stuffed up from crying. She was such an idiot. Snatching a tissue from the box on the nightstand, she pressed it to her eyes. How could she have been so dense? All the preparation, the nice dinner, the candles, her dress and hair had come to naught. Clay did not want her.

How had she made such a mess of things? She'd only

wanted to protect her heart, and instead she'd managed to wound herself beyond repair. Sighing, Tobie sat up and peered at her reddened face in the mirror.

Who was the woman staring back at her. A little more than a week ago, she'd been confident, self-contained Dr. Tobie Avery, engaged to one of the most prominent physicians in Fort Worth. Now she was an emotional wreck who'd dumped her fiancé for the unrequited love of a down-and-out inventor.

All those years she'd spent carefully planning her well-ordered future had disintegrated into a tangled mess. She'd never figured on falling in love with Clay Barton. From the very beginning, he'd represented everything she'd sought to avoid.

Then after her mother had talked to her and she'd discovered the fortune her father had left behind, Tobie had realized at last money did not count, that love and faith and loyalty were the things that mattered. She'd learned to accept Clay as he was, faults and all. Unfortunately she'd learned the lesson too late.

The unexpected sound of her door bell chiming had Tobie's spirits soaring. Was it Clay? Had he come to apologize? Quick as a cat, she sprang from the bed and hustled to the front door, flinging it open without hesitation.

Edward stood on her doorstep, a folder clutched in his hands. Disappointment surged through her. What was he doing here at this time of night?

"Hello, Tobie," he said coolly. "May I come in?"

"It's late, Edward."

He consulted his watch. "Only nine o'clock."

"I've hospitalized two patients, I have to make rounds at six-thirty." Funny how that excuse hadn't stopped her from planning an all-night romp with Clay.

"I've got some important information I thought you should know about. It concerns your new boyfriend."

"He's not my boyfriend," she denied.

"Then you don't want to know what I discovered?" Edward arched one eyebrow and waited. He dangled the folder tantalizingly between his thumb and index finger.

"Come in." She moved aside to allow him entry. Had Edward unearthed the secret Clay had so closely guarded? Anxiety thrummed through her veins at the prospect. Did she really want to know what he was hiding?

Edward stepped into the living area. Tobie perched on the edge of the sofa and motioned for him to sit down beside her.

"You know, Tobie," he said, after settling into the cushion and placing the folder on her brass and glass coffee table. "I've been doing a lot of thinking since you broke our engagement."

Tobie cleared her throat. She did not want to hear this. From the moment she'd first clamped eyes on Clay, had felt those strange stirrings generated by his intense stare, she'd known she had never loved Edward. "I thought you came to tell me something about Clay."

"I did, but I also wanted to let you know how much I miss you."

To spurn and be spurned all in one night. Tobie laid a hand on Dr. Bennet's shoulder. "It's over between us, Edward."

"Don't be so hasty, Tobie. Listen to what I have to tell you, then make up your mind."

She nodded. She'd hear him out, but she knew no chance existed that she'd ever get back with Edward, no matter what he might reveal about Clay.

Edward leaned forward and opened the manila folder, then angled her a meaningful look. "I was correct. I had seen your Mr. Barton before."

"Oh?"

"Inspect this." Edward plucked a picture from the folder and passed it to Tobie.

Holding it up to the light, she looked at the couple captured in black and white. The photograph depicted a younger Clay on the arm of the beautiful Nancy Freeborn, a known social climber who in recent years had married a wealthy older man and promptly shoved him into a nursing home while she made the social scene. Tobie had met her at several of Edward's fund-raisers and had disliked the woman on sight.

"So?" Tobie shrugged, feigning nonchalance.

"Just as I had surmised, your down-and-out inventor is actually the son of oil and gas magnate, Carlton Barton." Edward seemed to take a perverse joy in breaking this news to her.

Tobie studied the photograph again, absorbing Clay's appearance. He wore an Armani suit, expensive enough to give Edward a run for his money, and a Rolex watch. Clay's hair was neatly trimmed, his imported Italian shoes freshly polished. No doubt about it, the scruffy inventor she'd fallen in love with was really a jet-setting multimillionaire.

Nausea washed over her.

"I told you," Edward gloated. "Barton's been playing you for a fool."

Clay had lied to her. Why? What was the point? Unless...her stomach lurched at the possibility. Had he merely been playing on her sympathies, trying to get her into his bed?

But if that were true, why had he thrown her out of his apartment tonight when she'd been ready to give herself to him?

She felt completely betrayed. Even tonight, Clay had continued the sham, pretending that losing the patent for his invention spelled his failure as a man, when all along he was heir to a vast fortune. She didn't understand his convoluted game, but Clay Barton was a liar. How could she ever have thought she could love a man like that?

"Barton dropped out of the society scene four years ago," Edward intoned. "He denied money from his family, holed up like a hermit to 'prove' himself as an inventor. He's a kook, Tobie. He's not worthy of your attention."

But why didn't he tell me the truth? Tobie fretted. Why had he continued to hide his true identity from her? There could be only one answer. She meant nothing more to him than a passing fancy.

Her earlier sorrow at his rejection turned to hard, cold anger. How dare he treat her like that!

"What do you say?" Edward crowed. "The man lied to you. He toyed with your sympathies, recreating your failed relationship with your father. Subconsciously you saw Barton as a way to even things out with your father. He used you, Tobie. Face it."

She barked out a harsh laugh. Suddenly, all the riches in the world meant nothing. Without honor, integrity and honesty, money had no meaning. The bottom line was she couldn't trust Clay. And when it was all said and done, everything came back to trust.

"Are you all right?" Edward sounded alarmed.

"Oh, yes." An icy calm filled her veins. Despite the pain, she was grateful Edward had come here to tell her the truth about Clay. At last she knew the secret he could not reveal. She knew their relationship was doomed. It was over.

Tobie got to her feet. "Thanks for coming, Edward."

"That's it?"

"Yes." She walked to the door.

Reluctantly Edward stood. "Well, if you ever change your mind about us, you know where to reach me."

She forced a smile. "I think it's best if we don't keep in touch."

"Are you going to forgive Barton for lying to you?" Edward asked. "Please, Tobie, don't be a fool. Obviously the guy was out for all he could get. You didn't er...give yourself to him, did you?"

"Good night, Edward." The cool night air wafted inside her condo as she held the door open.

"If that's the way you want it." He stuck his chin in the air and sashayed out the door, leaving Tobie alone with her smoldering anger and her broken heart.

Clay sat in his jalopy outside Tobie's condo trying to work up the courage to go to the door. After he'd thrown her out of his apartment, guilt had gnawed at him relentlessly. It wasn't her fault he'd failed. She'd been trying to comfort him and he'd lashed out at her.

Taking a deep breath, Clay squared his shoulders and unsnapped his seat belt. Just as he was about to get out of the car, the door to Tobie's condo opened and Edward Bennet came strolling down the sidewalk.

His heart plummeted. Had she been crying on Edward's shoulder? Jealousy careened inside him like a runaway vehicle. The minute Edward climbed into his luxury car and drove away, Clay bounded up the steps, mentally rehearsing his speech in his head.

Reaching the door, he rapped loudly and tried to tamp down the anxiety knotting his muscles.

When Tobie didn't answer immediately, he tried again. "Tobie! Are you home? It's me, Clay," he called out.

A minute passed. Then another. He knocked once more.

"What?" she snarled, throwing the door open to glare at him. She was wrapped in a fluffy yellow bathrobe, her hair turbaned in a white towel. Her mouth was an angry slash. Even wet and mad she was sexy as hell. His eyes locked on the curve of her lower lip, and he had to fight to keep from kissing her. "What do you want?"

"I came to apologize for what happened back in my apartment. I was upset over the recycler."

Tobie folded her arms over her chest and glared at him. In the dimmed lighting her skin glowed white as the full moon hanging in the sky above them.

"Please," he said, unnerved by her stony silence. "Can we talk?"

At last she gave an imperceptible nod, turned and walked into the living room. She stopped, arms still folded, and continued to glare at him.

"There's something I've got to tell you," Clay confessed, "something I should have told you a long time ago."

She arched her eyebrows at him, still saying nothing.

Clasping his hands behind his back, he paced the length of her silver carpet. "I don't know where to start," he said at last.

She picked something up from the coffee table and handed it to him. "Does it have anything to do with this?"

Clay looked down at the photograph of him and Nancy Freeborn taken five years ago. So she already knew. That explained the silent treatment.

"Let me explain," he said.

"Please. I'm all ears."

He cleared his throat. "I'm not poor."

"Obviously." Her expression was cold, emotionless.

"But I live that way because I prefer the simple life."

Her blue-eyed gaze pierced straight through him. "Why did you lie to me?"

Clay squirmed. How to exonerate himself from this mess? He thumped the picture of him and Nancy with his thumb. "I didn't want a repeat performance of *that*."

She cocked her head and leveled him a frigid stare. "Yes?"

The lump in Clay's throat grew larger than his recycler. The vee of her bathrobe offered him an erotic peek at her soft flesh. He'd bet anything she was completely naked beneath the thick terry cloth material. His fingers ached to reach out and touch her. To feather his lips along her elegant neck. To taste her fragrant bouquet, to breathe in her floral scent. She roused in him a roiling passion stronger than the ocean's tide, more powerful than the moon's magnetic tug.

His thoughts tumbled back over the week they'd spent together with Molly. An exciting, fun-filled week that rivaled any roller coaster ride. The laughter they'd shared, the joy of his completion of the recycler, the pure fun of caring for Molly. And the wondrous sensation of kissing Tobie senseless. He couldn't live without her now. He had to convince her to forgive him.

"Nancy and I were engaged," he said. "Briefly."

"Go on."

"It didn't take me long to figure out what she was after. My money, my social standing. All the things my parents considered important but I didn't. I broke off the engagement when she laughed at my dreams of becoming an inventor, and I caught her in bed with another man. And Nancy wasn't the first woman who was attracted to me for what I could give her."

Tobie continued to look at him as if he'd crawled from beneath a rock.

He took a deep breath. "I decided to live like a recluse and work on my recycler. So I wouldn't be plagued by the Nancys of the world, I adopted a modest life-style. And it worked beautifully. For four years I toiled over the recycler, throwing myself into the project, mind, body and soul."

"That's still no excuse for not telling me the truth. I told you everything about myself. You knew of my mistake with Edward, of my problems with my father. But you never reciprocated. You kept a vital part of yourself hidden from me. I'd like to know why.''

"Hey," he said, suddenly irritated with her high and mighty attitude. She wasn't the only one hurting here. "From what I first saw of you, you were exactly the Nancy Freeborn type. How was I to know your quest for security was really a backlash to your impoverished childhood? For all I knew you were another gold digger.''

"Listen to me, Clay Barton. I never came after you. You were the one who showed up in my office. You asked me to stay in your apartment and help you with Molly. The whole thing was your idea straight from the start.''

He ducked his head, toed the carpet. "Well, I admit that by the time I realized you weren't like Nancy and I wanted to get to know you better, I needed leverage. After all, you were still engaged to Edward.''

"What are you talking about?" Tobie sank her hands on her hips and her bath robe gaped a little more.

God, how he wanted her! She was everything he'd ever dreamed of and more.

"It wasn't very honorable. I freely admit that.''

"What?" she snapped.

"I wanted to get you into bed," he replied honestly. "From the moment I laid eyes on you, Tobie, you did strange and glorious things to me. And when you came to me tonight, so sweet and seductive, offering me your virginity, it was all I could do to keep from taking you then and there.''

That got a reaction out of her. A telltale blush stained her cheeks.

"I still don't understand why you felt it necessary to lie.''

"Would you have agreed to spend the night in my apartment if you'd known I could afford to hire a nanny to take care of Molly?''

"No."

"See?"

"But you could have told me later," she said.

"I didn't want you to get mad at me and leave. In fact, I had intended on telling you the truth after I patented the recycler. I wanted to make my own mark in the world. I wanted you to be proud of me for who I was, not for who my parents are or how much money they have."

There. He'd confessed the truth at last. Breathing a sigh of relief, he caught her eye.

"So you perpetrated a hoax in order to mislead me."

"I wouldn't put it like that."

"All along your intentions were merely to seduce me."

"It started out that way, but when I got to know you, things changed." He took a step toward her but she quickly backed away.

"Please," she whispered. "Don't touch me."

"I'm so sorry."

"You'd better leave." She marched to the front door and threw it open. The night breeze carried in the smell of honeysuckle.

He nodded reluctantly. "Can I call you tomorrow?"

"I think it best if you don't."

"I can't accept that, Tobie. You're upset. Sleep on it. Consider giving us a chance."

"I'm sorry, Clay. I simply can't get involved with a man I can't trust."

He fisted his hands. "Tobie, I'll do whatever it takes to prove to you I can be trusted."

She shook her head. "It's too late for that."

"I never meant to hurt you," he whispered. But hurt her he had. "If I could change the past, I'd do things so differently."

Shifting her weight, Tobie stared at the floor.

What was she thinking? Why wouldn't she met his eyes? Then a terrible thought occurred to him. What if she had renewed her relationship with Edward? That would explain her behavior, her stubborn refusal to allow him time to prove his good intentions.

Clay cleared his throat. Just when he'd been about to tell her exactly how much he loved her, the insidious possibility of Edward's return to her life invaded his mind. What if she were truly in love with Edward? He'd look like an idiot confessing his feelings for her if she didn't care for him in return.

Jealousy like he'd never known zapped through Clay with deadly force. Cramming his hands in the front pockets of his jeans, he fought to control his unbearable anguish. Too bad relationships weren't like machinery. If they were, he could twist a few wires, fuse metal, reconnect the circuit. But hell, he had no idea how to mend a broken heart.

Tobie's hand rested on the doorknob. Outwardly she wore her calm facade, but inwardly she was shaking. He'd manipulated her with his lies, yes, but he had not taken advantage of her. She hadn't done anything she hadn't wanted to do, had in fact longed for more from him. And he had possessed legitimate reasons for his deception.

Basically she knew he was a good man, did she dare take the risk of loving him? One more tender word from him and she'd collapse into his arms. She yearned for Clay Barton with such a passion the intensity terrified her, but could she depend on him? All her old fears came back in a flood of doubt.

"I'm asking you to forgive me." He stood beside her, his hands in his pockets, his shoulders hunched forward.

"I wish it were that easy."

"Tobie," he said, "do you realize that if I walk out that door tonight, I won't be back."

She opened her mouth to speak, to tell him to stay, to profess her love for him, but years of conditioning cemented the words in her throat. Clay stood waiting, his gaze inscrutable.

"Well?"

"Uh...I...er."

"That says it all, doesn't it, Tobie. You still want your cake and eat it, too."

"That's not true."

"Isn't it?"

"No."

"Then tell me you'll forgive me."

Oh, how she longed to exonerate him, but she was so scared. What if he hurt her beyond repair? She'd never loved before, and she found the pain so horribly fierce.

"Well then, that's that." Pain flared in his eyes before he turned and stalked out the door.

Tobie stood there a moment, frozen. Come on you ninny, don't you dare let him get away, the voice in the back of her mind demanded.

"Clay," she shouted, springing into action. She raced down the steps just as he got into his car and started the engine. "Wait!"

But she was too late. By the time she reached the parking lot, his tires were squealing away into the night. Heartbroken, she collapsed to her knees on the asphalt.

"Clay, I forgive you," she sobbed, "please, please forgive me."

Crickets chirped. Honeysuckle rode the air. The full moon spilled its cold light on her weeping figure. Clay was gone, and she had been the one to chase him away.

Two months passed.

After that awful night in Tobie's condo, Clay had realized he could not go back to her until he had something tangible to offer—a job, a successful invention, a future to build on. He loved her too much to hurt her any further. So, working feverishly, Tobie never out of his thoughts for a moment, he invented baby latches. These miraculous latches were different from all others on the market because they allowed adults easy access to cabinets and drawers but they would not budge for curious little fingers.

The true test of his latches came when he kept Molly overnight for Anne and Holt, and the inquisitive infant was unable to climb into his cabinets. He'd easily obtained a patent, set up production of the latches and placed ads in parenting magazines. In a matter of weeks he sold over ten thousand units. That's when he got the idea for the Baby Business.

A service on wheels that would come to your home, offering complete "babyproofing." For a standard fee, he would install baby latches, put up smoke and carbon monoxide detectors, plug electrical sockets, erect baby gates and give a safety evaluation of the home. He loved the job. It offered him freedom yet provided a much-needed service. To his amazement, the business was a huge hit.

In just two short months, he had become an overnight success, and it was all thanks to Tobie and Molly.

But despite the euphoria of his accomplishments, he couldn't stop thinking about how he had failed. Losing Tobie Avery had been the worst thing that ever happened to him. During the past months, his love for her had deepened, ripening into a mature attachment that demanded commitment. He had to give it one more try.

One Monday afternoon, exactly two months after he'd last seen her, Clay decided it was now or never. On the pretext of promoting his babyproofing service, he borrowed Molly from Anne, bolstered his courage and drove to Tobie's office.

* * *

"There's someone here to see you," Lilly told Tobie.

"What?" Tobie asked, distracted, looking up from the stack of papers on her desk. She felt bone weary. It had been months since she'd last seen Clay, and the man still dominated her every waking hour. How long until he disappeared from her mind? How much more would she have to suffer?

Several times she'd driven past his apartment, trying to gather the courage to go inside, but she'd been unable to face him. She'd failed him. When he had needed her forgiveness and emotional support, she'd held on to her fears like a miser, refusing to relinquish her doubts despite the promise of a wonderful love. It would serve her right if she ended up a bitter, frustrated old maid.

And the windfall from her father's wacky investment hadn't helped a bit. Sure, she'd been able to pay off her medical school loans and her condo. She'd hired a nurse and bought new office equipment. But despite the money, she'd never felt so insecure in all her life, not even in those desperate times growing up poor.

"I said," Lilly repeated, rolling her eyes, "there are two old friends waiting for you in the lobby."

"Who is it, Lilly?" Tobie sighed, tucking a strand of hair behind one ear. "I don't have times for games."

"If you ask me," Lilly volunteered, "fun and games are exactly what you do need. Ever since that 'thing' between you and Clay went sour, you've been such a grouch."

"I didn't ask your opinion, did I?" Tobie snapped.

"I'm sending them back," Lilly retorted as the door swung shut behind her.

Letting out an audible breath, Tobie pushed away from the desk and got to her feet. Who the heck was waiting in her lobby? She certainly didn't feel like entertaining anyone.

She heard footsteps echo in the hallway, then inexplicably her heart did somersaults, just like it always had when Clay was near.

No. It couldn't be. Quickly she finger combed her hair and bit down on her lips to redden them. Please, she thought, please.

The door creaked. A baby cooed. Tobie swallowed past the lump crowding her throat and looked into Clay's loving eyes.

He filled the doorway, all man and muscle, Molly riding his hip like a princess on a pony. Tobie noticed the child's hair had grown a bit and now curled up on the ends. The baby beamed.

"Hi!" Molly exclaimed and clapped her chubby hands.

"She learned how to talk," Clay said quietly, his gaze never leaving Tobie's face.

"Clay," she whispered and raised a hand to her neck. "What are you doing here?"

"Uh, well..." He extracted something from his pocket and handed it to her. Puzzled, she took the plastic-wrapped package and stared at it.

"Baby latches," he said by way of explanation. "I invented them. In fact, I started a babyproofing service, and it's doing really well. I thought maybe you wouldn't mind displaying my brochures in your office."

She squeezed the latches in her hand. That was it? He'd come to get her to endorse his product? Crushing disappointment closed in on her. What had she expected after two months? His proclamation of undying love?

"Sure," she forced out the word along with a casual shrug. "Consider it done."

"Down!" Molly demanded, tugging at Clay's ear. Giving Tobie an embarrassed grin, he settled Molly to the floor. The child immediately toddled over to Tobie's desk and climbed into her chair.

"Is that all you needed?" Tobie asked, her tone unusually shrill. She just thought she'd been hurting these past months. Now, seeing him, hearing his voice made her agony at their breakup much much worse.

He took a step toward her. Tobie moved back. Their gazes locked. He hooked his fingers in the belt loops of his faded jeans, Tobie folded her arms across her chest.

"From the first moment I laid eyes on you I've always wanted more, Tobie," he said, low and throaty. "Haven't you realized that by now?"

"You stayed away for months," she whispered, desperately fighting the tears threatening behind her eyelids.

"You threw me out. I was never very good at expressing my feelings, Tobie. I'm much better at fixing things."

"I was wrong Clay, so very wrong. I should have trusted you."

"No, darling, it was me," he said. "I should never have lied to you. Love can't be based on mistrust."

Love? Had she heard him right? Did he love her?

"D-Does this mean you think our relationship can be repaired?" she stammered, scarcely daring to hope.

"Not by talking."

He took another step. This time she did not retreat. This time she was not afraid.

Clasping her hands, he laced his fingers through hers and tenderly bent her arms behind her back, inching her ever closer until their bodies melded from shoulder to knee. His cotton T-shirt rubbed her silk blouse, his rough denim jeans grazed against the soft folds of her skirt. Each contact point radiated a delicious heat.

His gaze swept over her features as if he were committing her to memory, his gray eyes darkening with unexpressed emotion. Then slowly he lowered his head and claimed her lips as his own.

A pleasant haze drifted over her as he deepened their

kiss. She felt that old sensation of rightness and knew that in Clay's arms was the place she belonged for the rest of her life.

His tongue slipped past her teeth, a warm heaviness grew in her breasts. Longing mixed with need, metamorphosed into desperate yearning. In the exotic aroma that was uniquely Clay Barton, she savored a taste that spoke of creativity, inventiveness and rock solid dependability.

"Tobie," he said. "I promise to take care of you. For now and always. As long as you're with me, you'll never want for anything. I promise, darling, one way or the other I'll always provide for your needs, financial and emotional."

"What are you saying, Clay?" She smiled up at him, her heart strumming with happiness.

"Marry me, Tobie. Be my wife. Bear my children."

"Oh, Clay," she sighed, lacing her fingers together behind his neck. "What took you so long?"

"I had to prove to you, to myself, that I was worthy of being a husband and father, that I was up to the challenge."

"I believed in you all along," she confessed. "It was my own mistrust that tore us apart. Clay, I'm so sorry for all the pain I caused."

"Shh," he whispered, gently kissing her forehead. "We're together now and that's all that matters."

"But we wasted those precious months," she fretted.

He chuckled and nuzzled her at the intersection of her neck and collarbone sending shock waves of delight bouncing throughout her body. "Guess we'd better get busy making up for lost time."

"I love you, Clay Barton," Tobie announced, speaking out loud for the first time the words that had been in her heart from the moment they'd met.

"And I love you, Dr. Avery." He held her tight. "What say we go back to my place and recreate that little scene you surprised me with on the day I lost out on the recycler patent? I can't believe I was fool enough to turn you away."

Tobie blushed furiously at the memory. "And I can't believe I was dumb enough to let you."

"Uh, you're not still involved with Dr. Bennet, are you?" Clay asked suddenly, a concerned expression crossing his face.

"Oh, no! Once I met you, I knew I'd never loved Edward. You, Mr. Barton, stole my breath away."

"Good," he said. "That's the way I like my wives, breathless and naked. Now all we've got to do is work on the naked part."

A loud thump drew their attention to Molly. She grinned at them, proud at having knocked Tobie's *Physician's Desk Reference* to the floor.

"I don't know, Barton, getting naked seems to result in babies," Tobie said, laughing. "Are we ready for a Molly of our own?"

"Why, darling, didn't I tell you? Babies are my business." And with that he kissed her until there were no more doubts.

* * * * *

Bestselling author

Joan Johnston

continues her wildly popular miniseries with an
all-new, longer-length novel

The Virgin Groom

Hawk's Way

One minute, Mac Macready was a living legend in
Texas—every kid's idol, every man's envy, every
woman's fantasy. The next, his fiancée dumped him,
his career was hanging in the balance and his future
was looking mighty uncertain. Then there was the
matter of his scandalous secret, which didn't stand a
chance of staying a secret. So would he succumb to
Jewel Whitelaw's shocking proposal—or take cold
showers for the rest of the long, hot summer…?

Available August 1997
wherever Silhouette books are sold.

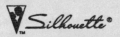

Take 4 bestselling love stories FREE

Plus get a FREE surprise gift!

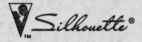

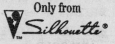

**Beginning in September
from Silhouette Romance...**

THE BRUBAKER BRIDES

a new miniseries by
Carolyn Zane

They're a passel of long, tall, swaggering cowboys who
need tamin'...and the love of a good woman. So y'all
come visit the brood over at the Brubaker ranch and
discover how these rough and rugged brothers got
themselves hog-tied and hitched to the marriage wagon.

The fun begins with
MISS PRIM'S UNTAMABLE COWBOY (9/97)

"No little Miss Prim is gonna tame me! I'm not about to
settle down!"
—Bru "nobody calls me Conway" Brubaker
"Wanna bet?"
—Penelope Wainwright, a.k.a. Miss Prim

The romance continues in
HIS BROTHER'S INTENDED BRIDE (12/97)

"Never met a woman I couldn't have...then I met my
brother's bride-to-be!"
—Buck Brubaker, bachelor with a problem
"Wait till he finds out the wedding was never really on...."
—the not-quite-so-engaged Holly Fergusson

**And look for Mac's story coming in early '98 as
THE BRUBAKER BRIDES series continues, only from**

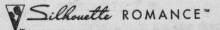

Silhouette ROMANCE™

BRU